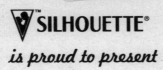

is proud to present

Night of the Dark Moon

Enjoy this incredible adventure in
the lush tropical atmosphere of Hawaii.

This mad dash through the impenetrable jungle
is almost the last thing a lovely photographer,
reluctant witness in a murder case, and her
hot-blooded bodyguard do.

Night of the Dark Moon

PAULA
DETMER RIGGS

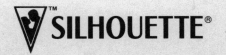

*Silhouette and Colophon are registered trademarks of
Harlequin Books S.A., used under licence.*

*First published in Great Britain 1993
Silhouette Books, Eton House, 18-24 Paradise Road,
Richmond, Surrey TW9 1SR*

© Paula Detmer Riggs 1992

ISBN 0 373 04646 4

54-9910

*Printed and bound in Great Britain
by Caledonian International Book Manufacturing Ltd, Glasgow*

Paula Detmer Riggs

I'm an only child.

Aha, you are now saying to yourself. That explains it. All only children are weird. Little hermits in training. Born recluses.

Alas, in my case that was indeed true. Not that I didn't have friends. I did. First it was *The Poky Little Puppy* and then later Nancy Drew and the Hardy Boys. I was content—until I was about ten and read *Gone With the Wind*.

It was stirring. It was thrilling. It was enthralling—until the end. When Rhett walked into the mist of Atlanta, I was devastated. Of course, that couldn't possibly be the way it happened, I told myself over and over.

Right? Right. Okay. So what did happen?

It took me weeks and weeks to devise an ending that suited me. I daydreamed through class after class, refining the he says and then she says, until, finally, I was satisfied. Of course, Scarlett got her man. With that firmly implanted in my subconscious, I could get on with my life.

Years passed. Reading was always my first love— until I met a certain adorable naval midshipman.

My first year composition prof told me that I had a gift for writing. Did I plan to become a writer? he asked.

My English lit prof gave me a C because I argued with him about Melville's use of symbolism in *Moby Dick*. What symbolism? I kept saying. It's a great example of storytelling, no more, no less. Good thing you aren't planning to become a writer, he sneered. Storytelling has nothing to do with literature.

I graduated, married my naval officer and kept on

reading through nineteen moves in five years. When first one hyperactive son and then another came along, I turned to storytelling to keep them quiet long enough to get clothes on them every morning. I told stories in the car to keep them safe. I told stories at night to lull them to sleep. When my boys were teenagers and no longer interested in stories, I went off to work. One day, I got fired.

Naturally, I went into a deep depression. I ate (mostly chocolate) and I read. After I'd gone through every book in our local library, I turned to the rack of romances.

From the first I was enthralled. I read while I cooked. I read late into the night. Hundreds and hundreds of romances I hadn't read. Soon I was haunting other branch libraries, searching for romances I hadn't read. At the time there were sixteen branches in San Diego. I soon had an intimate familiarity with all of them.

Ultimately, there came the day when I was reading faster than the authors could write. What did I do? Of course. I decided to write my own.

It wasn't easy. It wasn't particularly good, either. But it was the greatest high in the world when I finally finished. That book has never again seen the light of day.

My second, however, became a Silhouette book. The day I got the call remains one of my most cherished memories. I will be eternally grateful to my editor for opening the door to the most wonderful part of my life.

At last. The weird, chubby little girl with glasses who always had her nose in a book gets to make up endings happily ever after.

Paula Detmer Riggs

Chapter One

The sky was as black as a mourning cloak. Swollen clouds hung low over the Big Island of Hawaii. A *kona* wind whipped the Pacific to foam and tore at the coconut palms like an angry hand. The quarter horses in the main corral of Sinclair Ranch were restless, unable to settle. A storm was coming.

Alone in his office in the sprawling ranch house, Quinn Sinclair listened to the wind howl and thought about the fences that would need mending in the morning.

"Quinn, are you listening?"

Quinn tucked the phone receiver between his shoulder and ear. Bracing one booted foot against his great-grandfather's priceless koa wood desk, he balanced his chair on two legs.

"Sorry, buddy," he drawled in a voice that was still graveled from too many cigarettes at too young an age. "Storm's comin'. Might be a problem."

The man on the other end of the line snorted. "What about *my* problem? I didn't call you in the middle of the night here in D.C. to get a weather report."

"Hell, Eddie, I'd like to help you, but Meg handles the guest-ranch side of this operation. I just run the cattle on the working side."

"Don't give me that. You own the whole damn place. All...what? Two hundred thousand acres?"

Quinn stifled a yawn. His day had started before

the sun was even a glimmer in the east and wasn't finished yet.

"Something like that."

"So pull some strings with that sweet sister of yours and get Anne a room."

Anne. Was that the woman's name? Quinn hadn't been listening all that attentively. He was dead tired. His thigh muscles were beginning to seize up on him, and his back hurt. He'd been in the saddle from dawn for five days straight, riding fence and tallying beef.

In its heyday, Sinclair Ranch had needed a crew of forty *paniolos* to run it. Now he had nine, including himself. The payroll only stretched so far each month. From now until May, the height of the tourist season, he would be forced to make do with even fewer hands. Quinn rubbed the stubble on his jaw and thought of the ranch books he hadn't opened in three days.

"Problem is, Eddie, we only have twenty-five beds for paying guests, all of which, according to Meg, are taken for the next three months."

"What about the room next to yours? The one Candy and I slept in?"

Quinn's mouth thinned at the memory. Eddie's wife had come on to every man on the place. To him, too, before he'd let her know he wasn't interested.

"Give me a break, Eddie. The family wing's the only place I can go to get *away* from the tourists."

Five thousand miles away, in the icy slush of a Washington winter, Assistant Attorney General Edward C. Franklyn sat in a cluttered corner office of the Justice Department. In front of him was a thick file folder, marked with the yellow flag of the Witness Protection Program.

On the top was a candid photograph of a woman dressed in rumpled khaki shorts and an army-surplus shirt. Her hair was tousled, blond and naturally wavy. A camera of professional quality was slung around her neck, as much a part of her as the infectious grin on her face and the sexy little cleft in her chin.

Her name was Anne Oliver, age thirty-three, a freelance photographer of some renown. At the moment, she was Franklyn's greatest concern. Trouble was, his friend Quinn was a hard man to con, especially when it came to women. And Franklyn needed that room.

He decided to try another tack. "That's what I've been trying to tell you. The lady is almost family. One of Candy's best friends, in fact. They…work together in New York."

Deception was the one aspect of his job that he'd learned to tolerate but never liked—especially when he was forced to lie to a man he respected as much as Quinn Sinclair. Forgive me, buddy, he thought. Someday you'll understand.

"Tell you what, Eddie. I'll call around, get Candy's friend a reservation at one of the other resorts."

Static crackled over the line. Then Franklyn said, "Consider it a personal favor. Okay?"

Quinn heard the slight change in his old friend's tone. A favor, he thought. As in payback time?

His gut twisted before he controlled the surge of sudden emotion, just as he controlled everything in his life these days. Ed Franklyn had a right to ask a lot more of him than a room.

"What the hell?" he said, his voice resigned. "Let me know when the lady arrives, and I'll send the chopper to the airport in Hilo to pick her up."

"She'll be there at four o'clock tomorrow afternoon. And *the lady's* name is Anne Oliver. You can't miss her. Tall, blond. A real knockout."

"I said 'send,' Eddie. I don't intend to pilot the damn thing myself."

There was a pause. "I was hoping you'd take a personal interest in her. Show her around. Make sure things go smoothly."

Quinn dropped his feet and sat up. "Jeez, Ed, I'm a stockman, not an escort service."

"It's nothing like that, Quinn." Franklyn's voice took on a richer note. "Anne is special. She needs some...delicate handling."

"You mean she's a gold-plated bitch like...well, never mind who she's like. I get the picture."

Franklyn cursed the burst of patriotic zeal that had led him into government work. "Let's say I need you to put that temper of yours in cold storage while she's there and treat her like a VIP."

Quinn's gaze shifted to the wall that separated the two large bedrooms that made up the master suite.

A model, he thought. Tall and blond. No doubt she would have every hand on the place falling all over himself to light her cigarettes and saddle her horse.

"I'll make sure the lady has no complaints, Eddie. You have my word." He hung up before he changed his mind.

The DC-9 out of Honolulu landed in Hilo ten minutes early. Every seat was occupied. Anne's hope of a nap had been dashed when her seatmate had turned out to be a wispy octogenarian from Pasadena who was terrified of flying.

Even before the wheels had left the ground, Anne had found herself holding tight to the frail woman's hand. Every time the conversation had lagged, the woman had veered toward panic. Anne was nearly hoarse from the nonstop chatter.

The mood in the plane was lively as the soon-to-be vacationers slowly moved up the aisle. Even though the cabin was refrigerator cold, Anne felt as though she were sweltering.

As she made her way down the steps and across the tarmac to the terminal, she told herself to ignore the weakness making her muscles feel like twanging rubber bands.

Oliver women never fainted. It was so undignified. Heck no, Oliver women were of good Scottish stock—strong, stoic and certainly not given to embarrassing displays of weakness.

Trouble was, she didn't feel all that strong right now. Ten days in the hospital had left her pale and unsteady on her feet.

Inside the terminal, the waiting room was small and crowded. Tour guides with professional smiles dropped wilted leis over the heads of their wide-eyed charges before herding them into groups. Family members greeted each other joyously in a mixture of languages. Everyone seemed to have someone but her.

"Don't worry about a thing," Franklyn had said just before he'd put her on the plane at Dulles. "Quinn will take care of you."

At the time Anne had hated the very idea that anyone had to take care of her, let alone some reclusive stranger halfway round the world who thought she was someone she wasn't.

Her pale mouth curved into a self-conscious grin. A model, for Pete's sake. Someone who pranced on the wrong side of the camera lens. What the heck, Annie? she thought. You can do anything for two months. Right?

And then she would return to Washington, to a courtroom in the federal courthouse, to sit across from four vicious, sadistic killers who wanted her dead.

Anne's mouth went dry. Fear twisted in her stomach until she forced herself to relax.

So, she thought. Where are you, Mr. Sinclair? Tough-looking guy, Franklyn had said. Half Polynesian, from one of the oldest families in the islands. Big, he'd added, with diver's shoulders and a don't-bother-me look she was told to ignore.

"Hell of a place, that ranch of his," Franklyn had promised. "Very romantic. Popular with honeymooners. You'll love it. But you can't tell him why you're there. You can't tell anyone."

Feeling dizzier and dizzier, she scanned the features of a dozen men. More. None of them remotely resembled Franklyn's description.

Settling her bag more comfortably on her shoulder, she spotted an empty seat and headed in that direction. She was almost there when she sensed someone behind her.

The now familiar rush of fear tightened her throat, and she whirled. "What do you want?" she demanded.

Accustomed to men her own size, she found her gaze settling on a V of very dark, very soft-looking chest hair framed by the rumpled lapels of a chambray shirt that snugged powerful male shoulders and emphasized the breadth of a hard male chest. A blood-red lei was slung over one enormous shoulder.

She jerked her gaze upward. The eyes that raked

her face were too dark to be called brown, and yet they weren't quite as black as the silky lashes framing them. His hair, windblown and thick, was the same indefinable color that gave his eyes a suggestion of mystery.

His face was more angular than square, although his jaw had a stubborn jut. His skin was tanned a deep bronze. His mouth was resolute, strength trapped in the corners, misleading softness in the curve of his lower lip.

"Whoa, easy now. I didn't mean to scare you." His voice was slightly hoarse.

Anne's heart thrummed in her throat, and her hands were shaking. "Well, you did," she said, trying to regain her composure.

His mouth slowly formed a smile, as though the muscles of that part of his face were little used. "Sorry about that. I'm a little big to be sneaking up on anyone. I thought you saw me."

Anne felt a shadowy feeling of some elusive emotion pass through her. It seemed like desire. She was certain it wasn't.

"Let's forget it, okay?"

"Sure. I'm Quinn Sinclair."

The quick look he shot around and the subtle flex of his wide shoulders told Anne that impatience was as much a part of this man as the unknowable darkness in his eyes.

Feeling as though she was suddenly moving in slow motion, Anne forced her facial muscles into what she hoped was a friendly smile and extended her hand. "Call me Anne."

Instead of taking her hand, he took the lei from his shoulder and looped it around her neck. "Welcome

to Hawaii,'' he said before bending to brush a kiss
across the swell of her cheek. His lips were hard and
cool.

Anne felt her breathing change. It wasn't voluntary,
nor, she discovered, could it be controlled.

"Uh, *mahalo*. Thank you. And thank you for finding room for me.''

"No problem.''

Quinn had expected a beautiful woman. He hadn't
expected one with dark shadows under her eyes and
skin so pale it seemed almost transparent.

Her eyes, framed by curly wheat-colored lashes,
were a clear hazel without a hint of green. Tipped at
the outer corners, they had a sleepy cast, like a cat
too long in the sun. Her mouth had a soft look of
fragility that drew his gaze.

Her hair was sun-streaked, no doubt artfully done
every few weeks in one of those pretentious places in
Manhattan. At the moment it was pulled back into a
severe twist of some kind that made her look very
cool and sophisticated.

Champagne style and subtle vulnerability, he
thought. Class and a shimmering sensuality. It was a
hell of a combination. No wonder Ed had called in a
favor.

Tension began riding his spine. A heavy pressure
invaded his groin. The involuntary response made
him irritable. What a man couldn't control usually
ended up causing him trouble.

Two months, he thought. And she'll be sleeping
right next door. Terrific, Eddie. Thanks a lot.

"Ready? I want to get back to the ranch before
dark.''

"Mind if I collect my bags first?" she asked with the faintest suggestion of humor in her low voice.

His mouth twitched. "Not unless you make me carry them all."

"I've only got two and this." She touched the strap of her tote.

One of his eyebrows lifted. Anne had a feeling she had surprised him.

"This way," he said, nodding toward the corridor. He lifted her tote bag from her shoulder and hefted it over his. The purple-and-pink bag looked much smaller when he held it.

"Is your car outside?" she asked as she forced herself to keep up with his long, impatient strides.

"No, I brought the chopper."

Chopper. Anne's stomach lurched, and the little warmth remaining in her face turned to ice. She hated helicopters. "Is it far? Your ranch, I mean?"

"Twenty minutes."

Twenty minutes, she echoed silently. A lifetime.

An updraft caught the chopper, shaking it from side to side. Quinn adjusted the craft's trim and watched their shadow splash across the broad, open pit of Halemaumau. The ancient volcano, dormant now, but once a seething pot of lava, was like a beacon, guiding him home.

Polynesians had been on Hawaii for uncounted generations when Josiah Sinclair, a seaman from Maine on a whaling clipper, had jumped ship on his first trip to the islands, lusting for excitement and fortune. He'd found both, dying a wealthy man sixty years later.

Quinn and his sister, Meg, were the last of old Josiah's direct descendants. She had inherited the house. The ranch was his, the only thing other than his sister that he cared about.

Once, however, when he'd been eighteen, he had rejected his heritage and the responsibilities that went with it for a life at sea, just as Josiah had done.

He'd spent fifteen years as a Navy SEAL. Having barely scraped through high school, he began as a lowly seaman apprentice. But his own ambition coupled with a steely resolve to carry out every assignment to the best of his considerable ability had won him a commission when he'd been twenty-four.

Six years ago, after a stupid mistake had blown his career out of the water, he'd come home to heal, his soul and spirit battered.

He'd succeeded, but the cost had been a loneliness he'd learned to accept. At age forty-one, he was content with the life he'd struggled so hard to put back together again.

The only jarring note was the lack of funds that made it necessary for him to open the ranch to paying guests. Someday though, four, maybe five years by his calculation, he would have his mammoth debt reduced to a reasonable amount. And then he could return to the private life he craved.

He shifted in the hard seat and concentrated on the instruments. The sooner he got the lady to the ranch, the sooner he could get back to work.

Beside him, Anne managed another look at her watch. Ten minutes to go. Overhead, the rotors clattered and shook, jarring the breath from her lungs and battering her eardrums. Below her, Hawaii was a blur of green. Behind her were six empty seats.

Next to her, Quinn Sinclair slouched awkwardly in

the bucket seat that seemed too small and too low for his big frame. His long legs moved restlessly, as though the tension she felt in her tight muscles was somehow showing.

With the impersonal eye of an artist, she noted the flat belly and lean athletic hips, the soft, comfortable fit of worn denim over heavy thighs, the scuffed, dusty boots. Nothing fancy, nothing to impress. A working man's clothes. A working man's body. Strong, powerful, built for endurance and stamina.

Eyes slitted behind the traditional aviator sunglasses, he flew the ungainly craft with the reckless confidence of a combat veteran—or a man with a death wish.

A loner, she thought. Content with his own company. Not an easy man to like. But then, Franklyn didn't say she had to like him.

The chopper hit a spot of turbulence, tossing them upward and then down. "Oh," she gasped. Quinn glanced her way, catching her gaze on him. His mouth compressed, as though he were annoyed about something.

"Great view," she said, forcing a smile that felt transparently phony.

"See that crater?" he said into the microphone attached to his headset. "That's where Pele lives."

Anne looked down, her stomach lurching. She saw a deep conical hole in the midst of a barren moonscape. Surrounding the crater was a rippled ocean of gray lava.

"Pele was the goddess of fire, right?" she murmured, returning her gaze to Quinn's profile.

"Right. According to legend, she used a sharp stick to dig a hole on each island, which she filled with fire. But her older sister, Na Maka O Kaha'i, was jealous and filled each pit with water to put out Pele's fire.''

''Sibling rivalry, even among goddesses.''

One eyebrow arched above his dark glasses. ''Sounds like you have a sister.''

''Four, actually. I'm the oldest. I grew up on a farm in Missouri.''

Quinn could feel the friendliness radiating from her and told himself not to trust it. ''Just another all-American girl, I suppose?''

'''Fraid so. When I was growing up, they called us the Oliver girls. The mercantile used our picture to advertise back-to-school clothes. My poor daddy spent most of his money keeping us in dresses and shoes.''

''Is that where you got interested in modeling?''

''Something like that.''

Anne hated lying. Heat rose in her face, and she fervently hoped he wouldn't notice.

Something shifted in his eyes. What little warmth she had felt from him disappeared. She looked down, trying to see a house. A landing strip. Something.

Don't move, she told herself with false confidence as he guided the chopper lower. If you don't move, everything will be all right.

Without seeming to, Quinn watched the tip of her tongue run over her bottom lip. She was obviously terrified and trying hard not to show it. A sudden need to protect her caught him by surprise. He told himself to ignore it. He'd been trapped that way once before, and it had nearly destroyed him.

''There's the ranch,'' he said. ''On your right.''

She looked right, pretending an interest in the land

whizzing by beneath them. An irregular clearing had been cut into the trees like giant brush strokes of pale green crisscrossed by thin rust-red lines she took to be dirt tracks. Mountains rose on either side of the valley like ragged lines of crumpled black paper. At the far end a cluster of white buildings nestled in the shadow of the tallest peak.

According to Franklyn, the area was remote, unspoiled, even primitive in places. The inhabitants of the mountain villages still clung to the old ways and the ancient language. Time was relative, judged more by the sun and seasons than the clock. Secure as any safe house, Franklyn had promised.

Secure or not, she considered it better than the dreary bungalow in Maryland where they had tried to stash her. The tiny rooms and tall fences had made her stir-crazy. When she'd threatened to find her own hiding place, Franklyn, bless his heart, had come up with this one—if she didn't end up dead before she got there.

Anne took a deep breath, but the landing was perfect. Sinclair cut the engine and, while waiting for the rotors to stop spinning, efficiently carried out some kind of post-flight checklist.

One by one Anne relaxed the fingers mangling the soft suede handbag in her lap. Beyond the window she saw a huge white house that would have been ugly if it hadn't been so classically Victorian. Three stories high. Gabled, adorned with gingerbread on nearly every surface. It even had a turret, the rounded kind with a steep conical roof.

As she watched, an orange golf cart with a fringed canopy sped toward the chopper. The dark-haired, deeply tanned young man driving it wore a wild yellow-and-pink aloha shirt and white-duck pants.

Quinn removed his headset. He hung it on the hook under the window and indicated that Anne should do the same.

"Ron will take you to the house and get you registered."

Ron? The thought of facing yet another stranger was too much after a trip that had seemed endless.

"But I thought you…Ed said you would handle everything."

Quinn felt the contentment of being home evaporate. So Eddie had passed along his promise to give her the VIP treatment.

"Well, hell, Ms. Oliver, we sure wouldn't want you going back disappointed." His words had razored edges, but Anne was too exhausted to care.

He slipped from the seat and brushed past her to slide open the door. Anne followed, her balance precarious, her ears ringing.

He jumped down and extended his hand. Anne took it. Just as she stepped down, the scene in front of her began to whirl. The cement pad seemed to lurch. She had a sensation of tilting. Of hitting something solid. Of Quinn Sinclair's hard mouth forming words she didn't understand. And then…nothing.

She was on a bed. Not her own. The mattress was too soft. The air smelled different from her own town house in St. Louis, too. Something was wrong.

"Call the damn doctor, Meg. She's been out too long."

Anne turned her head toward the low, rumbling

voice edged with impatience. Sinclair. The sexy cowboy with the moody eyes.

"You heard what Eddie said when you called him," whispered a woman's voice. "She's suffering from exhaustion. That's why she's here—to rest."

In the dim light Anne saw Sinclair and a woman nearly as tall as he was standing by a long, narrow window. His sister? Wasn't her name Meg? Her usually excellent memory was strangely fogged.

Anne drew a deep breath. Life was returning to her body in stages. Fingers, toes. Arms, legs. Finally the rest of her.

"Why the hell didn't he tell me that to begin with?" Sinclair whispered, his voice rougher than Anne remembered. "Damn near scared me to death when she fainted."

"There's something you should know," Anne muttered, drawing their attention like the crack of a whip. "Oliver women never faint."

"Couldn't prove that by me," Sinclair muttered.

"Don't pay any attention to my brother," the woman told Anne as she came toward the bed. "He's not used to feeling helpless. And when you took that header into his arms, he didn't know what to do."

Quinn scowled. "Who do you think brought her here, then, if I'm so damn helpless?"

His sister ignored him. "I'm Margaret Sinclair, Meg to my friends," she said with a smile that twinkled eyes remarkably like her brother's in shape and color, but not in hardness. "I've been looking forward to meeting you. Eddie Franklyn is a particularly good friend of ours."

Anne tried to clear the cotton from her mouth. "I'm sorry I'm so much trouble."

Using her elbows, she pushed herself upward, only to discover, as the coverlet fell away, that her blouse was unbuttoned, allowing the lace and satin of her bra to show. That Quinn had noticed, too, was obvious after one hasty look at his face.

His eyes glittered with the kind of heat that was unmistakable. She averted her gaze, but not before she had seen the slow, sardonic lifting of one of his black eyebrows.

"Meg did it, not me," he drawled. "In case you're wondering."

"I wasn't," she snapped too quickly. She hated the heat climbing into her face. Oliver women never blushed. She forced herself to button her blouse one slow button at a time.

Meg Sinclair glanced from one to the other with a speculative look on her face that disappeared as soon as she returned her gaze to Anne's pale face.

"How do you feel?" she asked. "Are you hungry? Can Quinn get you a drink of something? Brandy, perhaps?"

Anne shook her head. "I'm fine," she said. "Just a bit jet-lagged." She pulled up the coverlet and made herself smile. "All I need is a good night's sleep."

A frown lined Meg's broad forehead. She was a stately woman in her late thirties with a look of compassion warming her smile. Anne liked her face. She liked Meg.

"Are you sure?" Meg persisted. "I could make you a sandwich."

"Leave the woman alone," Quinn interjected, a scowl pulling at the corners of his mouth. "She's a big girl. If she said she's fine, she's fine. Right, Ms. Oliver?" His gaze shifted to her face and stayed there. But his body still remembered the soft warmth of her breasts against his chest when he'd carried her into the house. For such a tall woman, she'd felt amazingly fragile in his arms.

Blood was pounding in her temples, and her face felt hot. She was beginning to feel off balance, the way she always felt when confronted with new and treacherous terrain. She didn't like the feeling. She wasn't sure she liked the man generating it, either. Just being near him made her jittery and tense.

"Right, Mr. Sinclair," she said. "But thank you for your concern. And your help. If I *had* fainted, that is. Which, of course, I didn't."

The look that flashed in his eyes was brief, but Anne had trained herself to look for the tiniest details that made her photographs unique. Amusement, she thought. The man can laugh. Why doesn't he?

"If you need anything in the night, just give a holler. I'm right next door." His gaze directed hers to a door to her left. It was closed. The ornate brass lock had no key.

"Next door?" she repeated. Fatigue buzzed in her head and slowed her thinking.

The sudden grin he gave her changed his face from interesting to dangerously attractive. "Yeah, didn't Eddie tell you? You and I are sharing the master suite. We're the only ones at the end of this wing."

He turned and walked toward the door leading to the hall. "Sleep well," he said as he went out and closed the door behind him.

Chapter Two

*G*unfire.

They had found her! She was going to die.

Anne jackknifed into a sitting position, her heart slamming against her rib cage. Brilliant light angled into her eyes, blinding her. Acting on instinct, she threw off the sheet and dove to the floor. Her elbow banged the hard wood, sending pain jolting through the newly healed flesh in her upper arm.

She cried out, then froze, flattened against the rough straw mat, face down, afraid to move. Afraid even to breathe.

What...? Where...? She looked around in a panic.

The big airy room with the old-fashioned furniture was quiet. Sunshine splashed the polished wood beneath her bare thighs and warmed her skin. Beyond the gabled windows, the sky was a clear, innocent blue.

There were no men in camouflage with automatic weapons. No protective FBI agents. No one in the room at all—but her.

And then she heard it, the clatter of metal on dirt. Horses' hooves.

"Terrific, Anne," she muttered into the woven floor covering beneath her cheek. "If you're a basket case now, what will you be like two months from now?"

Before she'd left the hospital, the doctors had offered tranquillizers for the rough times they told her to expect. Shakes, nightmares, extreme anxiety. Post-trauma stress, they'd called it. Common in gunshot victims. She'd refused the pills. Her emotions were sometimes too strong for her own good, but at least they were hers.

Needing to fill her lungs with fresh air, she hauled herself to her feet and hurried to the window. The panes opened outward, like old-fashioned casements, and she flung both windows wide.

Birdsong greeted her, along with the rustling of wind in the coconut palms. Beyond the neat fences, cattle grazed. Horses frolicked in the corral by a big white barn that looked more Yankee than Hawaiian.

The day smelled of something spicy. Ginger blossoms, maybe. Or plumeria. The dawn air was washed clean and felt cool against her bare arms. Below the windowsill, leftover raindrops glistened on the palmetto leaves, bright as crystal prisms.

She took another deep breath, then another, savoring the feeling of freedom. *You're alive, and it's a glorious, wonderful day,* she told herself. *Don't think about anything but enjoying it.*

It was early. The distant mountains were still shrouded in shadow. *Best shot in black and white,* she registered automatically, to show the dramatic silhouette of the peaks.

Closer to the house, however, she saw a montage of color. Exciting, vivid color—flowers, birds, even the clothes worn by the ranch hands in the corral.

In an instant her eye framed the picture. The men should be the focal point, with the horses they were saddling behind them. She would use fast film, a long lens.

Cowboys in Hawaii, she thought. Lean, wiry men

who looked tough enough to have stepped from the pages of the Zane Grey novels she'd devoured as a child. Their faces, burned to leather by the tropical sun, were a polyglot of racial mixtures, Hawaiian, Chinese, Japanese, Anglo—too many to identify.

Paniolos, they called them here. According to the guidebook she'd read in the hospital, the name came from the first Spanish cowboys on the islands. The cattle had come from Texas, gifts from Captain George Vancouver to King Kamehameha.

Very Hawaiian, she thought. English sea captain, Polynesian king, Spanish ranch hands. A blending of cultures, still dynamic and functioning, a hybrid blossom stronger than the root stock.

Perfect, she thought, excited at the possibilities. A story told in pictures. Her specialty.

She hurried to the bags lined up neatly next to a huge armoire. Last night, after Quinn and his sister had left, she'd unpacked the basics from the smaller bag, changed into her nightshirt, brushed her teeth and fallen into bed again. Everything else was still packed.

Eagerness welling inside her, she opened the larger bag and took out the only camera Franklyn had allowed her to bring, a vintage Nikon that looked anything but professional.

Purchased when she was thirteen with money she'd made baby-sitting, the Nikon was older than she was. It was a familiar weight in her hands. Her best friend. Sometimes she thought it was her only friend. The only one she could trust without reservation, anyway.

The camera was a part of her, sometimes the best part. Her way of forcing order into a disorderly world. Its eye, unaffected by emotion, was more sensitive than hers. Life was manageable when it was viewed through the length of a lens.

From the smaller bag she took a telephoto lens and fitted the two together. She slipped the old Nikon around her neck and returned to the window.

The onshore breeze caught her flaxen hair, whipping sleep-tangled strands into her eyes. She raised a hand to push it aside, and as she did, she caught sight of a rider cantering toward her across one of the fields.

He rode with one arm relaxed, the other holding the reins with an ease that made the powerful copper-colored stallion an extension of his will.

His straw Stetson was pulled low, hiding his features, but his skin was Polynesian dark and the hair that curled over his collar was as black as the stallion's mane.

It was Quinn.

She took a hasty step backward, reluctant to have him see her. Not that she was afraid, she told herself, even as her heartbeat took on a more agitated rhythm. Nor was she excessively modest, but she *was* standing there in a thin cotton nightshirt. And he was very male.

No doubt he'd received his share of "offers" from unattached female guests. A vacation fling was almost expected these days. For others, perhaps, she thought, absently rubbing the newly healed scar on her upper arm. Not for her. And certainly not with a man who looked as unbroken and dangerous as the stallion he rode. Right now, all she wanted to do was survive until April.

"Yo, boss," one of the men called out as Quinn approached the corral. "You got a minute?"

Anne didn't hear his reply, but the waiting men laughed, and one of them pushed open the corral gate, allowing the horse and rider to enter.

Inside, Quinn dismounted with the supple motions of a man used to the saddle. After removing his gloves, he tucked them into the low-slung waistband of jeans that had seen better days.

One of the hands took charge of the stallion, leading him into the barn. The others gathered around, talking and gesturing, respectful, but oddly boyish at the same time.

As Quinn listened, he swept off his Stetson and wiped his brow with his forearm. Even though he was surrounded by his men, he seemed apart from them. Not so much alone, Anne decided, as solitary.

Her natural curiosity took over. Was he a loner by choice or experience? Or did he feel superior to the men he commanded?

Perhaps, she mused. There was something intriguing about the set of his powerful shoulders that suggested an inner confidence and an innate toughness, the kind experience and struggle put into a person.

Still in shadow, Anne lifted the camera to her eye. With skill so practiced it was now instinctive, she framed the picture with meticulous precision until she got exactly the right combination of light and shadow.

An instant before she clicked the shutter, Quinn's head came up and he turned toward her. A hundred feet or more separated them, but the skillfully ground lens brought his face so close that she could see his mouth compress.

A scowl pulled his thick black brows into a V over the bridge of his nose, shadowing his eyes and reminding her of the storm clouds that gathered over the mountain peaks. His eyes narrowed, as though he were seeing her with equal clarity, although she knew that was impossible.

A sensation like warm water slid down her spine, and she snapped the picture. An instant later she stepped out of sight, the only part of Quinn Sinclair she wanted trapped forever on film.

The clock was striking seven when Anne descended the stairs to the main floor. She was dressed in white slacks and a long-sleeved yellow shirt, both old favorites.

The house was so quiet it seemed to be holding its breath as she reached the foyer and turned left, her sandals silent on the floor mats.

The lobby was deserted, the desk unattended. The plantation blinds were tilted upward, allowing light to enter but screening out the heat. The twittering of the morning birds and the nickering of the horses in the corral drifted in with the breeze.

The seductive aroma of strong coffee led her to a large airy room looking out on an exotic garden in full bloom. Tables set with flowers and damask clothes were cleverly scattered amidst flourishing plants as tall as small trees. The tables and chairs were empty. The room wasn't.

Quinn was standing in front of the massive nineteenth-century sideboard, pouring himself a cup of coffee.

He had discarded the hat and smoothed his hair into rough order. His shirtsleeves had been rolled another turn, revealing forearms corded with lean muscle. Sunlight streaming through the window turned the curly hairs on his arms to soft brown.

From the corner of his eye Quinn saw her come in. She stopped when she saw him, a look of uncertainty crossing her face. An instant later he caught a whiff of her perfume. It was subtle, making him think of spring rain and wildflowers.

Her long thick hair was braided and caught up by a frilly bow at the back of her neck. Sunlight found the lightened strands, turning them to gold. He was tempted to release that braid and watch the silk of her long hair fall loose against her neck. It would be slippery and warm against his rough fingers, like the rare lace ferns that grew only in the high country.

"Am I in the wrong place?" she asked. For the first time he noticed that she spoke with a faint accent. Not exactly Southern, but certainly not native New York. The cadence was easy on the ear. Perhaps too easy.

"No, just early," he answered. "Service starts at eight. Tourists sleep late."

"I don't mind waiting to eat, but I would kill for a cup of that coffee," she said with a hopeful look at the pot in his hand.

Quinn turned over another cup, found a saucer and poured. "Black, no sugar," he said before turning to look at her. It wasn't a question.

"Yes, how did you know?" Anne's voice was husky, and her breathing was too rapid, the only outward signs of nervousness she couldn't control.

"You look like a woman who takes her pleasures straight."

Pleasures. The word excited a dozen different images when he said it, all of them erotic. She told herself to ignore them.

"Hmm, a cowboy psychologist. I'm impressed,"

she murmured, fervently hoping that the heat blooming in her face wasn't visible.

"Naw, just a country boy, ma'am." He tilted his head and did his best to look humble. Anne thought he looked like a too-sexy, too-masculine little boy.

She burst out laughing. "I'll bet."

"True story. I learned to ride before I could walk."

"That I can believe. Your legs have that slightly bowed look."

His gaze dropped to the long expanse of soft, faded denim sheathing legs thick with saddle muscles. "The hell they are!" he grumbled.

Even as she grinned, she was admiring the symmetry of sinew and bone that formed his long, powerful body. Somewhere deep inside, something softened, like a sigh.

"Seems to me you'd be a good two inches taller if you could straighten those knees of yours," she mused. "Maybe three."

"Mainlanders. What do they know?" he groused. But he looked different somehow as he replaced the pot on the warmer, then spooned sugar into one of the cups. Younger, she thought. More relaxed. She had a feeling the boss worked harder than his men. Certainly he had been up earlier.

"Join me?" he asked, indicating one of the tables by the window.

"Thanks. Uh, *mahalo,* I mean." It had been a long time since she'd felt so…normal. It was a good feeling.

He carried both cups to the table, then stood by one of the chairs, watching her walk toward him.

The lady had style, he thought. No wonder she made her living showing others what to wear. Even though she was overdressed for the islands, the tailored outfit seemed absolutely right somehow. On her, anyway.

Her shirt, loose flowing and extremely feminine, brought out the gold in her almond eyes. Her slacks, cut in classic lines, bagged round the hips as though she preferred her clothes a size too big. Not that they detracted from the decidedly feminine curves they covered, he decided. Just the opposite.

His imagination was working overtime, trying to define the exact shape of her hips and thighs beneath the soft white material.

To Anne's surprise, he held her chair for her, seating her with impeccable courtesy before hauling out his own chair and settling into it.

Hidden sophistication, she decided. Rough on the outside, polished to a smooth hardness inside.

"You look better this morning," he said. "Your face has some color." And freckles spattered over her nose. Had the elegant model with the cool composure once been a tomboy, climbing trees and skipping rocks in a stream? he wondered.

She lifted one eyebrow and looked at him directly. "Why does that sound more like an insult than a compliment?"

His mouth, so hard a moment ago, took on a strangely vulnerable slant. "Maybe because I'm out of practice."

Anne wrapped her hands around the bone-china cup and waited for the hot liquid to warm her palms. "If you're out of practice, it's because you choose to be."

Quinn was surprised at the accuracy of her guess,

but he didn't let it show. "Probably," he said, his gaze falling to the snowy tablecloth.

"Why?"

Quinn wasn't used to directness in a woman. He wasn't sure he liked it. Or trusted it. "No time."

Anne tilted her head and studied him. His eyes were more brown than black in the morning light and edged with a circle of gold. She'd seen eyes like that before, on a rare Tibetan leopard she had stalked for weeks before getting close enough to capture the perfect shot.

Powerful, solitary, the big cat had tolerated her for reasons of his own. But he hadn't trusted her, even after weeks of familiarity. And when she'd gotten too close, he'd turned on her, wrecking her best camera and nearly mauling her before he'd suddenly changed his mind.

She shook her head slowly. "No, I don't think time is your problem."

"Hmm. Then what is?"

Sipping her coffee slowly, she thought about the dark, masculine features she had seen in the viewfinder. His face was lean, his nose aquiline, his bronzed skin stretched taut over strong bones. His mouth hinted at an elemental sensuality so powerful it bordered on frightening. His eyes compelled attention and, in some, obedience.

Aesthetically, his face was too harsh, too asymmetrical, too strong. Artistically, his face was a treasure, a portrait painter's dream. Or a photographer's.

But the man himself was an enigma. A rugged man of the land with rare moments of sensitivity and a hint of shyness. She sensed integrity there, and immense strength, the quiet unassuming kind that didn't parade itself for praise.

She was drawn to the man more than she should be. Excitement thrummed through her, and she tamped it down.

"You like women, but you don't trust them," she said over the rim of her coffee cup. "You don't trust me."

It had been a long time since anyone had read him so well. It made him edgy. "What makes you say that?" he asked before he could stop himself.

"Woman's intuition." And twenty years of studying faces.

He shifted in his chair, crooking an arm over the top rung and stretching out his legs. Dust still clung to the frayed jeans. His boots were worn down at the heels and scuffed at the toes, but the leather was first quality and the workmanship superb.

He looked up to find Anne watching him, a faint smile playing over her lips. The lady had a mouth made for kissing. Or was that an illusion, too?

He cleared a sudden thickness from his throat. "Eddie tells me you're a model."

He told me the same thing, she wanted to say. She didn't. This wasn't a game to be taken lightly. Her life was at stake.

"Yes, I'm a model."

"You live in New York?"

Anne took a sip of coffee. "When I'm not traveling. I spend most of my time out of the country." That, at least, was true.

Quinn toyed with his coffee cup. Usually he took his morning coffee in the kitchen with his sister and

Auntie Genoa, the ranch's chief cook. Bone china and linen tablecloths weren't his style.

"Ever been to Hawaii before?" he asked, because the silence unnerved him.

"Yes, about four years ago. But I never made it off Oahu."

"On a shoot?"

So he knew about modeling, she thought. Or at least the right word to use. Interesting. "Yes, on a shoot. In July, I think."

"Swimsuits, no doubt," he said, his mouth jerking slightly. Just thinking about her body dressed in little more than two scraps of material made his mouth dry and his groin hot.

"I wore a suit, yes," Anne admitted. But only because she had spent most of her time underwater, photographing the strikingly beautiful flora adorning the reefs. One of her photographs had won a prestigious award.

"Stayed at the Royal Hawaiian, I imagine."

Naturally, that was what he would expect of a highly paid model, she realized with a private moment of amusement. In fact, for most of her stay she had shared a room with her scuba instructor's twin daughters. They still exchanged cards at Christmas.

"Of course," she murmured.

"Nice life, if you like that sort of thing."

"I suppose I must."

One of his ebony eyebrows lifted slowly, and his expression clouded, as though he were considering her words. His very deliberation made her uneasy.

She turned her head and pretended to study the silent dining room. "This is a fantastic room," she murmured. "It has a friendly feel to it."

He looked around, his interest casual at best. "This used to be the solarium," he said. "My mother's favorite room."

"Is that Josiah?" she asked, indicating a large portrait hanging in a place of honor between two windows.

Quinn's gaze lifted to the thickly varnished portrait. Josiah Sinclair stared back at him, lines of wisdom etched into his austere Yankee features.

"Yeah, that's the great man himself."

Anne studied the face in the portrait. There was character there, she thought. And wisdom. But little kindness.

"You resemble him. Around the eyes, especially."

Quinn looked at the painting he'd seen every day of his life for years but never really studied. The portrait had been painted when Josiah had been well into middle age.

Crusty old bastard, he thought. Looked as hard as the Maine hills where he'd been born. Not a man a woman would take to if she had a choice.

His gaze returned to Anne's face and lingered. She had a quietness about her, a restfulness that he didn't expect from a woman who made her living in the fast lane. She had a way of relaxing a man just by sitting across from him. And exciting him just by lifting a cup of coffee to her full, soft lips.

"Family legend says that he jumped ship because he was about to be hanged for stealing the captain's rum. Took a keg with him, they say. Traded it to the first King Kamehameha for land and one of the king's stepdaughters."

Anne laughed. "That's terrible." She aimed another quick look at the stern face in the portrait.

"Shame on you, Josiah. I hope she ran you a merry chase."

Slowly she turned back toward Quinn. "Something tells me the man had a houseful of children."

"Eleven."

She grinned. "Good Yankee stock," she murmured. "How long were he and the chief's daughter married?"

Quinn lifted one eyebrow very slowly. "Who said they were married?"

Anne pretended to be shocked. "Is that why you're still a bachelor? Family tradition?"

"I'm divorced." Like a smothered flame, the glow that had appeared in his eyes went dark.

"Oops," she said. "I think I hit a nerve."

"It's been over for a long time." His voice was flat. Clipped.

Perhaps legally, Anne thought. But not emotionally. The residue was still there in the tension riding his shoulders and in the hard compression of his mouth.

"Sorry I brought it up. I'm way too nosy sometimes, mostly because I always want to know what makes people tick."

Quinn saw a look of concern cross her face. Did she sense the bitterness that his divorce had left him? Probably, he thought. She had a knack of slipping beneath a man's guard, enticing him to reveal far too much of himself.

In too many ways, the expensive model from New York wasn't what he had expected. Cool elegance one minute, fragile vulnerability the next. And now, consideration and charm, a potent combination. One that had trapped him once before—until he had discovered that those things, too, were illusions, created to entice.

What would she say, he wondered, if she knew that his distrust of women was caused by a beguiling, sensuous woman very much like her?

His hand reached out and captured hers. Ignoring her soft protest, he turned her hand palm up and studied the long slender fingers. They looked graceful and yet capable. Surprisingly, the nails were cut short and left unpolished. He liked the way her hand fit into his.

"You took my picture this morning," he said, lifting his gaze to her face.

The darkness in his eyes held her. Gray, she thought. Or black flecked with brown? Too many colors to label accurately, she decided. And far too expressionless for the violent emotion she sensed in him.

"Yes. If you like, I'll send you a copy when I… when the drugstore develops them."

Her gaze was direct. Too direct. He was used to evasion in a woman. And deceit.

He ran his thumb over her life line, and her fingers tried to close. Her wrist was delicately formed, with small bones and thin skin. Surprisingly dainty.

"Why take a picture of me?"

She felt strength in his touch. His hand was callused, the skin warm and dry, the easy control in his fingers absolute.

"You have an interesting face. Like Josiah's. I was curious."

He let his fingers play over the back of her hand. An urgency like the jittery feeling she felt in an electrical storm ran up her arm.

"Do you always get right to the point with a man?"

"With everyone. I find life more interesting when I don't have to deal with phony images."

Something stirred inside Quinn, a longing he'd thought dead a long time ago. He refused to trust it.

"Strange. Isn't that what you do for a living?" Sarcasm, quiet and suggestive, edged his voice. "Create phony images? Use sex to sell overpriced things to suckers who aren't smart enough to know they're being conned?"

Use sex. Anne's back teeth ground together. She had never used sex for any reason. Not in her work. Not in her personal life.

Oliver women never lose their tempers, she told herself. It's so exhausting. And sometimes very destructive, especially when it led to hurling things like expensive bone china at men who made insulting remarks.

Her gaze shifted to the cup and saucer in front of her, and her mouth took on a thoughtful slant. No, Annie, no, a voice warned. You like Meg Sinclair, remember.

Slowly, her eyes narrowing and her face freezing, she withdrew her hand and got to her feet.

"Thanks for the coffee, Mr. Sinclair. I'll see you around." Slanting him a cool smile, she turned and walked out of the dining room.

Chapter Three

Quinn couldn't remember the last time he'd slept past sunup. A few years back, probably, after one of the binges he used to go on when the rage inside him became too dangerous to handle sober.

Striding impatiently toward the kitchen and his first cup of coffee, he rolled one shirtsleeve another turn and started on the other. It was almost seven. No doubt his men would be wondering if the boss had tied one on again. Naw, fellas, he thought, the boss is just havin' trouble sleeping.

The kitchen door was closed. As he approached, he heard a burst of female laughter. It was a happy sound, but it only served to deepen his black mood. He hit the door with the flat of his hand, sending it flying inward.

Meg was there, and Auntie Genoa Kamae. He'd expected them. He hadn't expected Anne to be there, too, laughing with the others as though the three of them were fast friends.

Meg saw him first. "'Bout time you showed your face, big brother. I was beginning to worry about you."

Quinn's bad mood sharpened. "Don't bother."

"*Aloha,*" Auntie Genoa called out when she caught sight of him. Large of body and even larger of heart, Auntie Genoa always had a smile for the boy she'd helped raise.

She was coring pineapples for breakfast. Anne was

helping, eating almost as much as she sliced. She was dressed in a silky purple jumpsuit, with the pant legs rolled halfway to her knees, showing shapely ankles tanned a golden brown. Next to her suntanned skin, the rich color looked exotic and sexy.

Quinn felt the muscles of his jaw bunch. The kitchen was off-limits to guests.

"Morning," he muttered. His gaze met Anne's, and he nodded.

The violent emotion she had sensed in him was close to the surface now. Well hidden, to be sure, but she saw the signs. A slight narrowing of his dark eyes. Tension running along the hard curve of his mouth. A stillness in his face.

For two weeks she had stayed out of his way. Actually, it hadn't been difficult. She had learned very quickly that Quinn rarely mingled with the guests.

"Only under threat to life and limb," his sister had confided. "These days my brother likes his privacy."

Anne understood that very well. She, too, had a craving to be alone at times—to order her thoughts and listen to the quiet meanderings of her mind. But she also liked the company of others. Men, women, old, young—she had trained herself to discover something unique in each one.

"You were up late last night," she said, eyeing the deep lines in his face.

"Was I?"

"The floorboards creak," she said. "I heard you pacing."

Quinn allowed himself a brief look at her mouth. The corners were tight, but her lower lip promised a softness that most men would find irresistible. He felt a quick hit of desire surge through him and steeled himself to ignore it.

"Sorry it bothers you." He walked past her to the huge stainless-steel coffee urn that was always on, even in the middle of the night.

"We have a problem, Quinn," his sister said as he filled a mug with coffee. "The helicopter is out of commission."

"Since when?" The first swallow scalded his tongue, and he muttered an explicit obscenity.

"Sometime yesterday. Zach told me last night."

"Last night when?"

"Right after he made love to me. Not that it's any of your business."

Quinn felt heat climb up his neck. His sister and the ranch's pilot, Zach Hogan, had been lovers for years. He told himself he neither approved nor disapproved. It wasn't his place to judge. But he didn't much like hearing about his sister's sex life.

"What's wrong with it?"

"Something to do with the fuel line. Zach has to fly commercial over to Honolulu this morning for a part before he can fix it."

Quinn ran over the balance in the ranch account. This time of year, things ran close to the bone. "He'd better check with me before he spends any money."

Meg frowned. "We have to have the chopper, Quinn. Our entire activities program is planned around it. Today I was supposed to take a group to Volcanoes National Park."

"So plan something else."

"That, dear brother, was exactly what I was doing when you came barging in here. Anne has agreed to lead a photo safari."

"*Anne* has?" His gaze swung in her direction. "For a lady who makes her living on the other side of a camera, you take a lot of pictures. Half my hands spend more time getting haircuts than they spend working."

He leaned against the counter and crossed his legs at the ankles. Anne noticed that he was wearing another pair of beat-up jeans. The hem was frayed and the knees nearly worn through. His shirt was missing a button.

The man needed tending, she thought, then smiled to herself. He hadn't exactly asked for volunteers. Nor would she be first in line if he did. Still, the thought was intriguing.

Anne felt her cheeks warm and hoped he was too far away to notice the color that must be rising. "All models know a lot about lighting and composition," she hedged. "And photography has been my hobby for a long time." She nudged her chin higher. "Besides, since you won't let me pay for my room and board, I have to do something useful around here or I'll feel like a freeloader."

Quinn thought about the credit-card bills he was still paying down. And the divorce settlement that had all but put him into bankruptcy. He had learned the hard way that no woman ever gave a man something for nothing.

"Suit yourself," he told her. "Just stay away from my wranglers. They have better things to do than pose for pictures for a bunch of tourists."

"Thanks for the advice. I'll keep that in mind." Anne finished the last of the pineapple and began licking the juice from her fingers, drawing Quinn's attention to her lips.

She had the kind of mouth that made promises, even when she wasn't speaking. Promises that made a man hard and hurting. Promises that lied. Or did they? Suddenly he wasn't as sure as he needed to be. Uncertainty was new to him, and it made him irritable.

"I've got work to do." He drained his cup and rinsed it carefully, the way Auntie had drummed into him years ago.

He left without saying goodbye. A second later they heard the back door slam. Meg and Auntie Genoa exchanged looks.

"First of the month is a bad time for something to go wrong," Meg said.

"What's wrong with the first of the month?" Anne asked.

"That's when Quinn has to write out his alimony check."

Anne drew herself another cup of coffee. "I didn't think the courts awarded alimony anymore."

Auntie snorted. "They do when the wife hires a shark for an attorney."

"I could strangle that woman with my bare hands," Meg muttered, her voice seething. She caught Anne's eyes on her and attempted a smile. "In the old days a woman like that would have been stoned."

Anne lifted her cup to her mouth and drank deeply before asking in a casual tone, "Are you talking about Quinn's ex-wife?"

"Yes. Her name is Liz. Elizabeth Chesterton. Maybe you know her? She's a model, too. A friend of Candy's, in fact. Like you."

Auntie took another pineapple from the basket and

whacked it in two with a cleaver. "Nonsense," she snorted. "Anne and her are nothing alike. That woman never helped out a soul, 'lessen it was for money."

Anne dropped her gaze. "The name sounds familiar, but I don't know her."

"Just as well. She's a gold-plated bitch." Meg crossed to the stainless-steel refrigerator and took out a large bowl of eggs. From a shelf she took down another bowl. Anne lowered her cup and picked up an egg. Cooking wasn't high on her list of pleasures, but she did know how to scramble eggs.

"Why didn't he fight it? Offer a settlement instead?" she asked, tossing the shells into the sink.

Meg's smile had bitter edges. "He did. Or rather, his attorney did. She got that, too." She whacked another egg on the edge of the bowl, spattering herself and the counter with yolk.

"No wonder he doesn't have much use for models."

Meg stopped mopping the counter to eye her warily. "How'd you know?"

"From something Quinn said the first day I was here. I got the impression he didn't think much of...my profession."

"Don't take it personally, Anne. He's carrying around a lot of hurt. Has been for years. I'm not sure he'll ever get rid of it."

"I know," Anne said softly. "It's in his eyes."

"He makes me so mad sometimes!" Meg exclaimed. "As a kid he was unbelievably sweet in spite of that big, scary body. He didn't even date much in high school. Girls scared him, I think. I should have known he'd fall hard when he fell."

Yes, Anne thought. His feelings ran deep and strong. "How did they meet?"

"When he was in Newport for officers' training school."

"Worst thing that ever happened to him," Auntie proclaimed. "That she-bitch never would have married him if he'd still been an enlisted man."

Meg nodded. "That's for sure."

Anne wiped her hands and reached for her coffee, only to discover that her cup was empty. She moved past Meg to draw another cup. "Why did he leave the navy?"

Meg's mouth tightened. "He didn't. Not voluntarily, that is. They kicked him out."

Anne's hand jerked, spilling hot coffee on her fingers. "Ouch," she muttered, grabbing a towel. "Whatever for?" she asked, nursing her scalded fingers.

Auntie Genoa stopped chopping and looked at her thoughtfully. "You like him, don't you? I mean, this isn't just idle curiosity."

Anne frowned. Did she like Quinn? Or was she merely attracted to him? "No, I don't think I like him. But I...care about him. Does that make sense?"

Auntie looked sad. "Exactly how I feel about him these days," she muttered as she resumed her chopping.

Meg took a whisk from a hook overhead and began beating the eggs. "Quinn would kill us if he knew we were telling you these things. He doesn't talk about the past. Not ever."

"If you'd rather not—"

"No, I think you should know." Meg sighed. "I wish Zach hadn't made me stop smoking. I need a cigarette.'' She cast a hopeful look in Anne's direction.

"Sorry," Anne murmured. "I don't smoke."

"Smart lady." Meg paused, then said in a quiet tone, "Quinn and Liz had been married about eight years when he left for one of his special super-secret assignments. He was gone six months. When he got back his adoring wife was eight weeks pregnant."

Anne's eyes filled with pain. "Not by him, obviously."

"Obviously," Meg echoed in a dry tone. "Liz swore that she'd been raped by another officer, a friend of Quinn's."

"Oh, no," Anne murmured, her cup frozen halfway to her mouth.

Meg banged the whisk against the edge of the bowl, shaking off the last of the beaten eggs. From the rack over the stove, she took a huge frying pan and slid it onto one of the front burners.

"Quinn's always had a temper. Over the years he'd learned to control it, but this time he couldn't. He went after the guy. Put him in intensive care. Nearly killed him. Navy investigators arrested him for attempted murder. He was court-martialed."

Anne was too stunned to say anything. Meg's brief smile told her that she understood. "It was a circus. Your friend, Ed Franklyn, was Quinn's attorney. He put enough doubt in the board's mind to get Quinn acquitted of attempted murder. But the navy gave him a dishonorable discharge for striking a superior officer. He was lucky he didn't end up serving time in the brig at hard labor."

"And his wife?"

"She divorced him. Turns out she'd been cheating

on him for years and finally got caught. Her lover refused to accept responsibility for the baby, which apparently made Liz panic.''

''She lied?''

Meg nodded, her eyes growing stormy. ''She knew that Quinn had a temper. She used it to get back at her boyfriend.''

Anne groped behind her for the counter and tried to steady her shaking knees. ''Oh, my God.''

''He came home a changed man. Rarely talked, never laughed, kept to himself mostly. If it hadn't been for the ranch, I'm not sure he would have made it. Trying to make this place pay again saved him.''

Auntie nodded. ''Poor boy was in a bad way for a long time. First year he never left the ranch. Looked like he never slept more'n a few hours. A lot of nights he drank too much. But gradually he started putting himself together again.''

''You're right,'' Anne said emphatically. ''Some-one should have strangled the woman.''

Meg burst out laughing. ''I like you, Anne. We think alike.'' She hesitated, then added, ''You would be good for Quinn. He needs a woman like you.''

''Hold on! He doesn't even *like* me.'' Anne felt her face warm and rushed to add, ''Even if I were inter-ested in him, which I'm not.''

''He likes you,'' Meg said.

Anne looked down at her toes. ''Could have fooled me.''

''That first morning you were here he had Manola saddle a horse for you. He'd planned to take you rid-ing after breakfast, and that's something he'd never done with a guest—not even once in the four years we've had the place open to tourists.''

Anne lifted her gaze and searched Meg's face. "He never said...I didn't know."

"Like I said, Quinn's always been shy with women. He was probably working up to asking when you walked out on him."

Anne's jaw dropped. "How did you know?"

Meg hopped down from the table and picked up her clipboard. "I was just coming down the stairs when I saw you charge out of the dining room. A few seconds later Quinn followed, looking as though he was about to explode. He slammed out of the house so fast the windows rattled."

Meg filched a piece of pineapple from the now brimming bowl and gave Anne a knowing grin. "I'm glad Eddie pulled strings to get you here, kiddo. If anyone can shake my big brother out of that deep freeze he's been in for so long, it's you. I'd bet my half of the ranch on that!"

Anne returned her grin, but her eyes were thoughtful. "Don't," she warned. "I wouldn't want you to lose."

The silence was magical. Anne rested her back against a smooth, cool boulder and watched the afternoon sun play over the velvet grass. The perfume from the flowers surrounding her was intoxicating. The breeze was gentle, scarcely disturbing the peace of the secluded grotto she'd come to consider her own private sanctuary.

A few yards away, Sadie, the spirited pinto mare Manolo had reserved for her exclusive use, grazed contentedly. Hummingbirds drank from orange flowers shaped like tiny trumpets, and butterflies of all sizes painted the air with color.

Anne pulled up one leg and rested her chin on her knee. All day, even as she had talked to a group of her fellow guests about light and shadow, composition and structure, she had been thinking of the things Meg had told her earlier. Dishonorable discharge. Even the words hurt.

"You're going to get wrinkles if you keep frowning like that."

Anne turned so quickly she felt a twinge of pain in her neck. Less than twenty feet away Quinn sat astride his big bay, watching her. Sadie nickered, acknowledging the presence of the two dominant males.

"Wrinkles don't bother me," she said, hugging her knees. "They give a person character."

"Character, huh? Is that in fashion these days?"

"It's always in fashion."

Quinn shifted in the saddle. One hand rested on the saddle horn; the other gentled the nervous stallion.

Anne found herself fascinated by those hands. His fingers were long and lean, the veins fanning the back prominent and strong, his wrists thick with muscle. And yet, when he tended the stallion, his hands were as gentle as a woman's. She raised her camera and snapped off a series of shots.

Quinn frowned and tugged his hat lower. "Meg tells me your picture safari is a hot ticket. You're booked solid for tomorrow."

"I had a great bunch of students. It was a kick."

His black eyebrows rose slowly. "Yeah, well, I thought you were supposed to be resting instead of working."

"Teaching isn't working. It's fun. I haven't felt this relaxed in years. No wonder you love it here."

Stillness froze his face. "Who says I do?"

"Don't you?"

Instead of replying he dismounted. The stallion shied, suddenly nervous, but Quinn held him easily. "Whoa, son. Let's you and me take a break." He led the stallion to the far side of the glen and tied him to a sturdy bush.

"What's your horse's name?" Anne asked as Quinn walked toward her.

"Kanaloa."

This time her smile was spontaneous and genuine. "That's perfect. Did you name him?"

He nodded. "He's named after—"

"—the Polynesian god of the underworld," Anne finished for him. "Some of the books call him the 'devil-god.'"

Quinn hesitated, then sat down on a large flat rock and extended his long legs in front of him. He swept off his hat and wiped his damp forehead with his forearm.

Anne caught a whiff of sweat and dirt—rough, masculine scents that should have been distasteful. Instead, she found the combination oddly exciting.

"Been reading up on local history, have you?" he asked as he tossed his hat aside.

"Of course. Usually I do that before I…travel to a place, but this time I…the trip was arranged in such a hurry." Anne watched speculation settle in his eyes and rushed on. "I know there are four main gods. Ku, Kane, Lono and Kanaloa."

She smiled at the dubious look crossing his face. "Kane is the most powerful, since he's the one who created the world by using the seeds from a calabash. Seeds for the clouds and rain and wind. Other seeds for the stars and the moon and the sun."

She lifted her face toward the warming rays and inhaled slowly, savoring the mingled scents that were so strong they were almost intoxicating. She heard the wind in the lacy branches above and the rhythmic swish of the horses' tails. It felt good to be alive. To be safe.

"Right?" she asked, turning toward Quinn.

He inclined his dark head in a brief nod. "What about the mountains and valleys?"

Frowning, she searched her memory. "Those he made from the flesh of the gourd."

"So they say."

He seemed relaxed, but his eyes were guarded. Now that she knew why, she wanted to tell him that she understood, but instinct told her that would be a mistake. A man as proud as Quinn would mistake empathy for pity.

He rested his elbows on the rock and leaned back. His frayed shirt pulled taut over his lean belly. Anne wondered how those hardened muscles would feel against her palm.

Before she realized what she was doing, she snapped off several more shots. Of the lazy glint in his eyes. Of the play of light and shadow over his powerful torso. Of the taut disapproval flattening his mouth.

She lowered the camera and rested her elbows on her knees. "Then along came Lono. He was a farmer at heart and also, I think, a poet. Anyway, he's the one who made the flowers grow and the grass green. He's the one who created the delicious smells and colors and tastes that make the islands so special."

Something changed in Quinn's eyes. The blackness seemed to shift, revealing an emotion that she had

never seen before. Before she could define it, however, his silky lashes wiped it away.

"You have a good memory."

"I also enjoy immersing myself in the essence of
a place. It helps me...in my work."

At the mention of her work, his head came up
again, and she saw that the hard measuring look was
back in his eyes. "What about Ku? Did you read
about him?"

Anne leaned back and rested both palms on the
cool grass beneath her. "Now that guy was the problem. For some reason, he decided that this beautiful
paradise needed people to enjoy it. So he created man,
and all the troubles that man brings to a world."

Quinn found that he was looking at her mouth
again. The softness drew him, tantalized him, teased
him. "Funny. I thought the trouble didn't start until
he created woman."

"Spoken like a true Polynesian chauvinist," she
said.

"Half-Polynesian."

"*Hapa-haole,*" she echoed. "Half-white."

"Yes." The terseness of his answer didn't surprise
her. From the three or four times they'd been together,
she had learned that he rationed his words even more
rigidly than his smiles.

Anne plucked a handful of grass and let it sift
through her fingers. Across the glen Kanaloa suddenly
snorted and pricked his ears. Two squirrels, chattering
madly, chased each other through the drooping leaves
of a giant bird of paradise.

Without thinking about it, Anne caught a picture
of their romp. When she lowered the Nikon again,

she found that Quinn was watching her with a strange look on his face.

"Do you ever go anywhere without that thing?" he asked, indicating the camera.

"No. It helps me understand things around me."

"The camera never lies, huh?"

"Not to someone who is willing to look honestly."

She shouldn't be so easy on the eyes, he thought. But she was, with her hair tossed into wildness by her ride and her eyes half-closed with the pleasure of the day.

His pleasure was more basic. He wanted to be inside her, those sleek thighs locked around him, her sweat drying on his skin.

He shifted his position, but the heaviness in his groin remained. A man could lose his soul to a woman like that if he wasn't careful.

"What does your camera tell you about this place?" He trailed his gaze around the grotto.

"That it's safe here." She glanced his way, catching a look of surprise in his eyes. Speculation.

"Safe?"

Alarm shivered through her. He was coming too close. And close meant danger. In more ways than one, she realized.

"I mean, it's very special, very spiritual. This particular place is very old, but time has no relevance here."

He sat up and let his folded hands dangle between his knees. "You must have been talking to my sister."

Anne felt a chill. "About what?"

"This is an ancient *heiau,* a temple, where the people came to pray."

To pray. Was that what she'd been doing? Praying for strength? For courage? For Quinn's deep wounds to be healed?

"So that's why it's so peaceful here," she murmured, lifting her shoulders and letting them fall.

"Legend has it that the *kahunas,* the priests, are still here."

"Is that why you come? To pray?"

"Not anymore," he said, rising. He leaned down to retrieve his hat and put it on.

Anne sensed that their time together was ended. She scrambled to her feet and brushed bits of grass from her seat.

"Time I was leaving, too," she murmured with a trace of regret. "I promised Mrs. Bronsky I'd be a fourth for bridge this afternoon."

"Sounds like fun." His tone suggested that he thought it was anything but.

"Bridge isn't your game, I take it."

A shadow crossed his face. "Too tame."

Quinn walked with her to the spot where Sadie had been waiting patiently. The mare snorted when they reached her side and nuzzled Anne's shoulder, eager for another run.

Anne laughed and produced a carrot from the pack strapped around her waist. "Half now, half when you get me safely back to the barn," she said as she broke the carrot in two.

"This old girl's gonna be sorry to see you go," Quinn said with a chuckle. "Manolo tells me you've got her as spoiled as a pet and about as tame these days."

His hand smoothed the pinto's mane. Anne's stomach fluttered.

"I'm not sure about that. She tossed me on my bottom this morning."

He looked down at her, a trace of worry moving across his face. "Something scare her?"

"Yes, a barking dog. How did you know?"

His hand came up to finger a stray lock of Anne's hair that curled against her neck. "Since she was a foal, she's shied at sharp noises. That's why Manolo has orders never to let novices or children ride her."

His fingers brushed the thin skin beneath her jaw. Fire spread from the spot. "She didn't go far," she murmured.

"She never does."

"She's been trained well."

"Yes."

It seemed so natural to lift her gaze to his. He took a step closer. Or perhaps she moved first.

"I'd better go," she murmured, even as his thumb began a gentle exploration of her cheek.

"Not yet." His fingers flattened against her jaw. It seemed so right to tilt her head toward his touch.

He lowered his head a few more inches until his mouth was slanted directly over hers. "God help me, I have to do this," he whispered. Before she had a chance to refuse, his mouth took hers.

Sudden, unexpected sensations jolted through her. Surprise, desire, a promise of something even more powerful.

At first he merely tasted, exploring her mouth slowly, thoroughly, with his. His lips were warm and coaxing. Perhaps she could have withstood a demand, but the sweet persuasion of his surprisingly gentle kiss was more difficult to resist.

She swayed, suddenly unsteady on her feet. He

kept the kiss soft and lingering, but his hands stole around her, holding her gently, as though she were very precious to him.

Needing to touch him, she smoothed her palms up his arms to his big shoulders. His powerful body shuddered, as though it had been a long time since he'd been touched by a woman.

He pulled her closer, but the camera hung between them, keeping them apart. With a growl of irritation, he lifted it over her head and hung the strap on Sadie's pommel. The mare snorted and tried to nose between them.

Quinn grinned, even as he concentrated on her mouth again, this time with the urgency of a desperately lonely man. The shock of the impact shimmered through her, and her fingers tightened on his arms. His mouth brushed hers, lifted, returned with more pressure.

His lips were warm, his body warmer, but she thought only of his mouth. Of how it was making her feel. Of the desire building in her.

His tongue moistened her lips, sending slow waves of pleasure rolling through her. Her heart thudded in her chest as his arms tightened until his lower body was aligned with hers. Denim pressed against denim. The hard evidence of his growing need pressed against the softest part of her belly.

Her legs went watery, and she clung to him, her fingers pushing against hard, lean muscle. Gradually, skillfully, he deepened the kiss until her pulse was roaring in her ears.

Fire flickered inside her. Did he feel the heat in her? she wondered.

She went on tiptoe, trying to get closer. To get inside that place no one was allowed to know.

Quinn felt his body swell to full arousal and his control waver. He had known desire for a woman, but he had never felt driven to take and take and take until he was filled with the taste of her and the feel of her and the warmth of her.

He traced the line of her soft mouth with his tongue, his heart hammering violently against his rib cage. Trapped behind the fly of his jeans, the hard bulge she had caused throbbed to the point of pain.

Every day, since seeing her in the terminal at Hilo, he'd wanted to taste her soft, impudent mouth. Every day he thought about stroking the satiny skin that grew tanner and tanner. Every day he tried not to notice the long sleek thighs and rounded bottom. And every day he failed.

He ran his hand down her back to cup the tight buttocks that teased him into a foul temper every time she paraded across the yard in those damn tight jeans.

He had known that her body would fit perfectly against his. Soft curves, long graceful angles. Neatly, perfectly, and yet not submissively.

God help him, he wanted to take her here in this sacred place, where such things were forbidden. He wondered how he had lived so long without her.

Locked against him, Anne felt his body rock against hers. Hard, insistent, distinctly male. Small darts of need shot through her, and she moaned.

Quinn heard the small helpless sound and knew that he was close to crossing the line between choice and demand. He was sliding into quicksand with this woman. In another few seconds it would be too late.

He jerked his mouth from hers. He was breathing hard. So was she.

Anne slowly opened her eyes and looked up at him, the hazel depths soft with the same need that was throbbing through him. He saw no hardness in her, no calculation, no coy pretense. Because he wanted to believe that so desperately, he knew he couldn't let himself take the chance.

"Aren't you going to stop me?" he demanded, his eyes feverish with a hunger he was powerless to hide.

His harsh tone hit her like a sudden torrent of icy water. The temper she told herself she didn't have fought with an acute wave of disappointment.

"Yes, I'm going to stop you," she said, twisting out of his arms. "And don't ever do that again."

She turned, but before she could mount, Quinn lifted her in his arms and deposited her in the saddle as though she weighed no more than air. He gathered the reins and put them in her hands. He wasn't smiling.

"Don't ever give a man like me orders," he warned, his voice graveled. "I'm the one with the key to that damn door between us, remember?"

Before she could answer, he swatted Sadie on the rump and the mare surged forward. All Anne could do was hold on.

Quinn was alone, a bottle of rum at his elbow, a glass in his hand. Moonlight filtered through the blinds, leaving stripes like prison bars on the age-darkened floor of his bedroom.

"Here's to celibacy," he muttered, pouring the last of his drink down his throat. The liquor was rough, burning all the way to his gut.

He reached for the bottle and refilled his glass. The clink of glass on glass reminded him of nights better forgotten, nights spent in this room alone, a loaded pistol in front of him offering relief from the humiliation burning in him.

Tonight, however, it wasn't the past tormenting him. It was Anne Oliver. The taste of her. The feel of her. The soft look of desire in her golden eyes.

In his office, when he should be working on the books, he found himself remembering the light in her eyes when she talked of her feelings about the *heiau*.

In the pasture, when he should be on the lookout for strays or busted wire, he found himself wishing she was there to watch the sunset with him.

In this room, with only a door between them, he found himself hard and aching with a need that he couldn't seem to banish, no matter how many cold showers he took.

He kept remembering her in the grotto this afternoon. She had made him see his land in a different way—the way she saw it. Enchanted. Special. Enduring. And she had made the ancient legends come alive again.

He had known her only a few weeks, spoken with her only a few times, yet he was always aware when she was near. He scarcely knew her, yet he sensed that he changed when she was around.

She raised longings in him that he'd thought he'd put aside years ago. Longings that made him want to trust again. To trust in the things he saw in her eyes.

With one quick movement he downed the last of the drink before slamming the glass down on the desk. At the same moment the ornate Victorian clock that had been a housewarming gift to Josiah and his bride from Kamehameha tolled the hour.

Midnight.

Biting off a curse, he left his bedroom and headed for the wide, curving staircase where five generations of Sinclair wives had waited for their husbands. But no one waited for him.

His long, saddle-toughened legs took the stairs two at a time, the thudding of his heels muffled by the runner. The foyer was illuminated by the moonlight shining through the etched glass.

He jerked open the door, leaving it ajar behind him. Lava stones crunched under his boots as he headed for the barn. Moments later he emerged astride Kanaloa.

He gave the stallion his head, and Kanaloa bolted, heading for the treacherous trail leading to the foothills. The wind, spiked with the first drops of the storm, lashed Quinn's face as he galloped into the waiting blackness.

Chapter Four

*T*hey were big, brutal men in camouflage, silhouetted against the edge of the precipice. Two in front, unarmed, hands raised. Four behind, with rifles.

Cold winter daylight dulled the ice crystals carpeting the hard ground. Drab gray clouds pressed down.

"No!" Anne screamed. "Don't!"

Her cries were obliterated by the explosion of gunpowder. The men in front jerked, their bodies absorbing slug after slug. Blood spurted, congealing in the frigid air.

The echoes of the shots faded. Silence settled. The rifles aimed toward her. Fear spiraled, clutching at her throat. Her legs were leaden, her breath icing into vapor in front of her.

She turned and ran. Her Jeep was in sight when a bullet caught her in the arm. She spun crazily, pain spiking hot in her flesh. She managed to jerk open the door, start the engine, drive. She wouldn't die. Not here. Not like this.

"No," she choked. "I won't. I won't."

"Easy, Anne. Relax. It was just a dream."

Rough but gentle fingers stroked her cheek, bringing warming blood back into the icy flesh. Still swimming toward consciousness, she turned toward the comforting touch. Beyond her closed lids she sensed light. Warmth. Safety.

After an eternity, she managed to open her eyes.

Quinn was sitting on her bed, wearing only his jeans. His face was lined with tiredness, and those unreadable black eyes were rimmed with red.

The connecting door was open. Beyond, she saw a massive bed and rumpled sheets. The pillow was indented where his head had lain. No doubt the crisp cotton was still warm from his body.

His nearly nude body, she realized, taking note of the broad, bare shoulders and the massive chest furred with soft, dark hair arrowing to the waistband of unbuttoned jeans.

"I have this dream... It's so aw-awful."

Like vivid photographs, the images haunted her. The faces of the two men. Their eyes. Their mouths open, screaming. They hadn't wanted to die. No one wants to die. Not like that.

She began to shake. Her teeth began to chatter. "I'm not u-usually like this," she murmured. "I'm always so g-good at...at coping, but this..." She broke off, her gaze clinging to his. "S-sorry. This isn't your problem."

Quinn hesitated, then lay down beside her and took her in his arms. Before she could draw a breath, she found herself cradled against his wide chest.

Anne stiffened. "Quinn—"

"Shh. Go back to sleep."

Anne murmured a protest and tried to sit up. Quinn's arms tightened. She tried to hold herself separate, to hang on to her need to be brave. But the heat of his body was like a sedative, enticing her to relax. The scent of soap clung to him, clean and reassuring. His furred chest rose and fell in a hypnotic rhythm, lulling her.

Her lashes drifted closed, her cheek resting on his

wide, smooth shoulder. His big hands began combing through her hair, spreading it across her back like a silky fan.

She snuggled closer, cushioned by the lean, hard muscles beneath her. Her arms curled around his waist, and her lips curved into a drowsy smile against the downy chest hair tickling her nose.

"I just figured something out," she murmured.

"What's that?" Even half-asleep, she knew that his voice held a smile.

"Deep down, under all those frowns and bad temper, you're really a very sweet man. I'm glad Ed sent me to you."

His hand stopped moving, and he seemed to stiffen for a moment before his fingers burrowed into her hair to rest on the sensitive spot at the nape of her neck. His touch was intimate and yet nonsexual, the touch of a friend more comfortable with actions than words.

"Go to sleep, Anne," he ordered in a gruff voice. "I'll keep the nightmares away."

She smiled. "I wish you could. But you can't."

A few minutes later, she was asleep.

In the half-light of dawn, Quinn lay motionless, cradling Anne against him. She was using his chest as a pillow, and her hair was a soft blanket warming his skin. She was asleep, her breathing even and quiet.

Moving slowly so as not to wake her, he raised one arm and tucked his hand under his head. He hadn't intended to fall asleep. A man was vulnerable then, especially in someone else's bed.

Quinn inhaled slowly, intensely conscious of the soft feminine body curled against his. Until his marriage, he'd never spent a night with a woman without making love to her.

With Anne, everything was different, especially the need he felt to be with her. Awake, asleep. Talking, not talking.

She had a way of reaching down inside him and pulling out things he had vowed to keep hidden. And that scared the hell out of him.

The mistrust his ex-wife had put in him was still strong. He wasn't sure if anything or anyone, even Anne and her soft smiles and willing kisses, could exorcise it.

Slowly he eased from beneath her and rolled out of bed. He went into his own room, clsoing the door quietly behind him.

He was halfway to the bathroom and a cold shower when the phone by his bed buzzed. The blinking button indicated his private line.

"This better be important," he snarled into the receiver.

"It is."

Quinn recognized Ed Franklyn's voice. He also recognized the deadly urgency in his tone. He sat down on the bed and rubbed his morning beard. "What's wrong?"

"Are you alone?"

Quinn glanced at the closed door. "Yes."

Silence hummed over the line, broken by intermittent static. Quinn waited, his gaze narrowed and his mouth hard.

"There's a problem," Franklyn said, breaking the silence.

"I'm listening."

Huddled in a phone booth three long, cold blocks

from his office, Ed Franklyn stared at the swirling flakes of snow hitting the glass. His eyes were bloodshot, and his tongue was fuzzy from the endless cups of coffee he'd drunk.

"You remember when I told you I had taken a job in the Justice Department after I retired from the navy?"

"Something about immigration statutes, wasn't it?"

"Not exactly." There was a pause before he added, "I'm in charge of the federal Witness Protection Plan."

It took Quinn less than a second to realize his old buddy had used him. "Anne," he said in a cold, clipped voice.

"I've always said you were quick."

"Not quick enough, apparently. You set me up."

A weary sigh hissed along the line. "It was necessary."

"That's crap and you know it."

"I know how you feel about that ranch of yours, and I was afraid you would have refused if you thought the place might get shot to Swiss cheese."

"You've got that right." Quinn drew a calming breath, reining his temper tight. "Tell me about Anne."

"Have you ever heard of the Aryan American Brigade?"

"Vaguely. Neo-Nazi bunch of idiots, aren't they? Hate-mongers?" Quinn stared at the red ball that was the rising sun.

"Exactly. Currently based in Colorado. Our best estimates put their numbers at close to twenty thousand, divided into cells located mainly in the western states. Their leader is an ex-marine named Marvin Draygon.''

"I've seen pictures of him. Charismatic son of a bitch.''

"Yeah, along with being ruthless and vicious and hell-bent on destroying anyone whose pedigree doesn't come out white Anglo-Saxon Protestant.''

The muscles of Quinn's spine tightened. "What's Anne got to do with bastards like that?''

"Well, first off, she's not a model. She's a free-lance photographer. She was doing a piece on a species of endangered deer in some godforsaken place in Colorado when Draygon and three of his lieutenants took a couple of FBI undercover agents into a field and turned their AK-47s on them. Anne saw it all.''

Quinn muttered a vicious curse. "No wonder she has nightmares.''

"What's that?''

"Nothing. Go on.''

"Because of her, we have a good chance of convicting Draygon and his buddies of first-degree murder. Trial starts April second—if she lives to testify.''

"If?"

This time the silence was tense. "We had a female agent acting as a decoy in a Silver Springs safe house. Looked enough like Anne Oliver to fool her grandmother.''

"What happened?''

"Six bastards in full combat dress got past two of the Bureau's best. Killed the decoy and split, but not before they got a good look at her face. They know she wasn't Anne Oliver.''

Quinn bit out another vicious curse. "Get somebody here. *Now.*''

Franklyn's voice turned defensive. "We're working on it."

"Not good enough," Quinn shot back, his voice instinctively taking on the steel of command.

There was another silence before Franklyn admitted, "We have reason to think there's a leak in our secure network. If we send someone to get her, they might follow."

Quinn's hand gripped the receiver so tightly the plastic nearly cracked. "What do you want me to do?"

"Fly her to Pearl Harbor in your chopper. Turn her over to Navy Intelligence. They can take care of her until I can make secure arrangements."

Quinn stared at the sunshine spattering the floor, his stomach slowly twisting into a hard knot. "The chopper's out of commission. Busted fuel line."

"Coincidence?"

"Probably," Quinn conceded. "You want to bank on that?"

Franklyn's reply was obscene and to the point. "Any ideas? I'm fresh out."

Quinn closed his eyes and visualized the island he knew as well as he knew his own body. "There's a small patch of deserted beach on the Hamakua Coast between Keokea Beach and Waipo Bay. We take the guests there sometimes to snorkel. It's rough country, no roads. You have to get in by sea or air."

"Spell those two names for me."

Quinn obliged, then continued, "I'll have her there at dawn on Thursday."

"But the chopper—"

"We'll go by horseback."

"Horseback? That seems damn risky, Quinn."

"Don't worry. The country between here and there is about as wild as it gets. I have relatives living in places in the hills that the *haoles* and the other tourists don't even know exist. Once I get her there, we should be safe enough."

There was a pause before Franklyn said curtly, "Sounds workable. I'll make the arrangements. I'll be coming to get her myself, so she won't be scared spitless."

Quinn stared out the window at a sky that seemed an innocent blue. "What about Meg and the others?"

"Odds are the Brigade doesn't know where she is. Even if they did, I doubt they would chance another all-out attack."

"I can't risk my sister and the others on a guess, Ed. Get some protection out here."

"As soon as I can. In the meantime—"

"In the meantime I'm posting men in the house. They'll be visible, and they'll be armed."

Franklyn sighed. "One more thing you should know, Quinn. Ms. Oliver took a bullet before she managed to get away from Draygon and the others. God knows how she managed to survive, but she did. We can't lose her now."

Lose her...

Quinn went deadly still. His eyes took on the texture of slate. "You won't lose her," he said. "Count on it."

"I will." There was a pause before Franklyn added tersely, "Let's keep all this just between you and me. She's a gutsy lady, but she's already been through one trauma. We need her wits about her when she testifies."

"That's damn cold-blooded, Franklyn."

"It's my job."

"It's still lousy." Quinn hung up and headed for his closet. From the top shelf he took a large brown metal box. Inside were his service medals, his lieutenant-commander's shoulder boards—and the piece of paper condemning him to live the rest of his life with shame in his gut.

His mouth tightened, but his hand was steady as he pulled out the worn holster containing his father's .45 and a box of ammunition.

Chapter Five

Anne lifted her face to the shower spray and let the hot water cascade over her. She sudsed herself slowly, her thoughts turbulent.

Quinn had slept with her. He hadn't made love to her.

She was grateful. She was also, she discovered, disappointed.

After the kiss in the glen, she'd stopped pretending that she wasn't sexually attracted to him. She was. Intensely. So much so that she couldn't stop thinking about that hard, nearly naked body next to hers. So much so that she was soft and aching inside.

The few serious relationships she'd had had been on her terms, controlled as carefully as the composition of her photographs. But that would be impossible with Quinn. No woman controlled him. She doubted if anyone, woman or man, ever had.

Impatient with her own thoughts, she threw back the shower curtain and reached for the towel. Through the open window she heard the now familiar sounds of the ranch coming to life. Horses neighing. Pickup trucks clattering down the lane. Deep male voices calling out morning greetings.

Finished drying, she drew the towel around her like a sarong. Her skin was still damp, but the air was warm. Humming to herself, she tucked one end of the soft terry between her breasts before she left the bathroom.

Two steps into her bedroom she stopped short, a soft gasp of surprise escaping her lips. Quinn was standing by the dresser, rummaging through the top drawer.

His jaw was freshly shaved, his hair shiny and clean, his clothes slightly less disreputable than usual. Little shivers of awareness took over her stomach and tightened her throat. Did it show? she wondered. The hot, fluid need he aroused in her?

"Looking for something?" she managed.

The raw, pink scar on her arm hit Quinn hard and low, like a sucker punch. He wanted to wrap her in his arms and promise to keep her safe. He wanted to kiss the violated flesh until pleasure obliterated the memory of the pain she had suffered. He did neither. It was safer that way—for both of them.

Returning his gaze to the open drawer, he shoved a handful of silky underthings into the worn saddlebag looped over one arm. The flimsy garments seemed very fragile in his big hands.

"We leave in ten minutes. Better hustle." He closed the top drawer and opened the next. He pulled out two shirts and began stuffing them in the bag.

"Just where is it we're going in ten minutes?" she asked.

"To a wedding luau."

"I must have missed the part where we discussed this."

Her shower cap was still wet. Drops of water were beginning to dribble onto her forehead. With an impatient frown, she pulled off the cap, allowing her hair to cascade to her shoulders. Quinn watched without moving, but inside, low and deep, he felt a ripple of desire.

"Wear jeans and boots," he ordered. "And a hat. It's a day's ride there, a day back. Plan to spend the night."

He tried not to notice that the skin above the skimpy towel was still dewy from her shower.

"No, Quinn. Thank you, but...no," she said, allowing a trace of impatience to show. "I promised Meg I'd lead another photo safari this morning."

Quinn watched her chin take on that slight tilt he was coming to recognize as determination. The lady certainly had her share. But so did he.

"That's not a problem. The chopper is fixed. Meg won't need you after all." The lie came hard, but Quinn told himself it was necessary.

He closed the drawer, slung the bags over his shoulder and came toward her. He stopped an arm's length away, his expression revealing little.

"Take your camera along to the luau if you like. There will be traditional food and dancing, the way it should be done, not the watered-down show Meg gives the tourists. Most *haoles* never get a chance to see something like this. Most wouldn't even notice the differences. You will."

Anne hesitated, poised to voice another, stronger refusal. But the lure of witnessing a genuine island celebration conducted in the age-old way was nearly irresistible. Even so, a night with Quinn was sure to test what little resistance she had left.

She forced herself to meet his eyes. "About last night..."

"Last night you needed a friend," he said, his voice bare of emotion. "I was the only guy around at the time."

The bed they had shared was only a foot away. She knew it was there. So did he.

"And tonight?"

"Tonight is up to you." One quick step closed the distance between them. "But I won't pretend I don't want to make love to you, because I do."

His hand came out and hooked around her neck. At the same time his mouth descended, opening over hers in an unmistakable demand.

Anne stiffened, but the resistance she tried to summon melted into the pleasure jolting through her. Her lips softened under his.

His fingers flattened along her neck—not quite caressing, and yet no longer controlling. His free hand pressed against her back, arching her toward him until their thighs met.

His thumb stroked the soft skin above her breasts, sending urgent darts of sensation deep into her. She pushed against him, rising to her toes so that she could feel more of that hard mouth. Her hand caught him behind the neck, her fingers digging into the thick ropes of muscle. His hair felt surprisingly silky, almost too soft for such a hardened man.

A groan rumbled from him, and his body surged against her. Only a towel and a thin layer of masculine clothes separated her skin from his.

Heat rushed through her. Yes, yes, she thought. Nothing seemed to matter but the flood of wonderfully warm, tingling feelings surging through her.

Her body was fluid, pliant, ready to mold to his. His was hard and thrusting and blatantly aggressive. She moaned at the thought of being filled by him.

His tongue dove deep, and she met it eagerly with hers. He probed; she suckled. His hand pressed her spine, forcing her closer, closer, until she felt his heart beating a violent rhythm against her breasts.

His mouth lifted, and his hand released the pressure on her spine. Anne swayed, her lips still parted and moist from his mouth. Her skin felt hot, and her breathing was erratic. Her hands clutched the slipping towel.

"Here, let me," Quinn said, replacing her hands with his. He snugged the knot tighter, his fingers brushing her breasts. The nipples hardened, showing clearly through the soft towel.

Quinn's eyes changed until they seemed to smolder. "I want you, Anne," he said in a rough voice that was more demand than plea. "But the choice is yours. I won't force you."

He brushed her mouth, then stepped away. "I'm leaving in ten minutes. Are you coming?"

Anne ran her tongue over her tingling lips. He waited, a stillness in his eyes, the tension in his face drawing her. The distance was there, the wall that he put between himself and the world, but something was different. Something important. Something inside him. But what?

"Yes," she said with a smile that trembled only slightly. "I'm coming."

"Welcome to Kaliwea," Quinn said as they entered a large clearing that seemed to have been scraped by a giant hand out of the side of the mountain. By Anne's watch, it was a few minutes past four.

They had been riding most of the day. At first the trail had been clearly marked. But now there was no trail at all, only the one in Quinn's head.

With each mile they'd traveled, they had gone

higher, and the air had become thinner, the foliage thicker. Anne felt hopelessly lost.

Overhead, the sun was hot, but they were sheltered from its rays by a cooling canopy of trees. The shade, a dark emerald, smelled musty, like freshly plowed earth after a rainstorm.

"Is this part of the ranch?" Anne asked as she guided Sadie onto the rutted lane.

"Used to be. I sold it to Mama Chloe a few years back."

"Is she our hostess?"

"Yes, my father's second cousin. She's a self-taught expert on traditional Polynesian culture. Has this thing about preserving the old ways before they're gone forever. She intends to build a replica of an ancient village up here. Bus in the tourists. Put on authentic dances. Serve traditional food. Tonight you'll be sleeping in a hut with a grass roof."

"Sounds like fun."

His gaze flicked her way. His eyes seemed to smile, and Anne wondered if she was imagining it.

"Don't get too excited. Primitive life means no indoor plumbing and no electricity."

"Oh."

"Don't worry. Mama wants her guests to come back. She's made a few compromises with authenticity."

Anne looked down at her dusty jeans. "Thank goodness," she muttered.

Quinn laughed. It was the first sign of relaxation, of trust, she'd wrung from him. She wanted to shout for joy at the special gift he'd given her. She wanted to be in his arms.

Silly, she told herself. It was just a laugh.

They rode slowly, the clatter of the horses' hooves mingling with the call of birds and the whisper of the wind. On three sides they were surrounded by lush screens of overgrown brush. Directly ahead lay a large brown bungalow on stilts nestled in a grove of giant tree ferns.

Six steps led up to a wooden veranda, where handmade chairs with brightly flowered cushions were lined along the front facade. Under the veranda's weathered floorboards, plump chickens sporting exotic plumage in iridescent shades of bronze and green scratched for grain. Anne raised her camera and snapped off several frames.

"We'll pasture the horses here," Quinn said as he swung from the saddle.

Anne started to do the same, then winced at the stiffness in her thighs. Quinn tied the stallion to a sapling and then, to her surprise, lifted her to the ground.

"Sore?" he asked, his hands lingering at her waist.

"A little. It's nothing serious," she said. Her heart was pounding in her throat, making it difficult to speak.

He hesitated, then removed her hat and hung it on the mare's saddle horn. "I like your hair better the way it was this morning."

One twist of his hand and her hair fell free of its neat coil, brushing her neck and cascading over his wrist. His fingers lightly massaged the nape of her neck, evoking sensations of pleasure and warning.

"When you first arrived, I knew you were going to be trouble." His gaze was searching. The dark centers of his eyes were flecked with the gold of some powerful emotion.

"I don't mean to be."

He moved closer until his chest was only a deep breath away from her breasts. His hand exerted pressure, forcing her face to tilt toward his.

"When you cut me off at the knees that first morning, I thought you were playing hard to get."

She saw the tension in his face and the restraint he imposed on the firm mouth that looked as though it wanted to smile.

"I don't play games," she murmured, her voice too husky.

One side of his mouth angled upward, drawing her gaze to the lips that refused to yield to a smile. "I know that now. I don't, either."

Her mouth went dry. "I know."

Anne lifted a suddenly trembling hand to his chest. Her fingers clutched his shirt. To push him away? To pull him toward her?

He waited, his breath warming her lips. All she had to do was turn her mouth aside, she realized with sudden certainty, and he would stop. She knew, too, that he would withdraw from her then. Utterly. Irrevocably.

He wasn't a man who gave second chances. Not to himself. Not to anyone else.

"Quinn," she whispered, her mouth meeting his. To her surprise, he kept the kiss brief, almost chaste. His hands framed her face, keeping her from getting closer. She frowned, her breath coming too fast, too hard.

Just then the door opened and people spilled out. The screen door slammed, and Anne jumped, her heart racing and her eyes going wide.

He lifted his mouth from hers and turned them so

that his body was sheltering her. "I've always had lousy timing," he muttered.

Anne was suddenly conscious of the intimacy of his thighs and hers. She stepped back and tried to brush some of the wrinkles from her shirt. "Are...are they all your relatives?"

"'Fraid so." Without seeming to, his gaze swept over the group, looking for unfamiliar faces. He saw aunts, uncles, cousins and cousins of cousins. No strangers. Some of the tension left his braced muscles.

Large and small, adults and children, they whooped and hollered as they ran toward them. Anne heard his name. Other words.

"Aloha," they called in ragged unison.

"Aloha nui," Quinn answered, besieged by hugs and kisses.

He did his best to introduce Anne to everyone. He used her first name, nothing more. Island friendliness? she wondered. Or a gesture, signaling that she was to be treated like more than a friend?

She shook hand after hand, trying to match names with faces, engulfed in a sea of welcome. Their surprise at seeing Quinn was obvious. Their surprise at seeing her was even more so. But their clamorous delight in having their reclusive cousin visit more than made up for the initial awkwardness.

Loni, the bride, was short and plump. Her eyes were soft and shy, but her excitement was almost palpable. To Anne's amazement, she discovered that the bridal reception, the luau, preceded the actual ceremony that was to be held at noon the next day.

"You sure you want to do this thing?" Quinn asked his cousin as he enfolded her in a bear hug.

"Are you kidding?" Loni returned with a mischievous grin. "It took me three years to land that stubborn man of mine. I'm not going to give him up."

Quinn shook his head. "Poor Cully's in for a hell of a life, I can see that."

Loni slapped at his shoulder, but she was still grinning as she turned to shyly acknowledge Anne's good wishes. "I'm pretty nervous, I have to admit."

Anne smiled. "Would you mind if I took your picture? And pictures tomorrow, of the wedding? As my gift to you and Cully?"

Loni's eyes shone. "Are you a photographer?"

Anne felt the blood rush to her face. "Uh, I work with cameras a lot in my career."

"I'm told that Anne is a model," Quinn put in, watching Anne's face. "Right, Anne?"

"Right," she said, feeling sick inside. She stepped back and framed the shot. Loni wet her lips and fluffed her hair, looking pleased and uneasy at the same time.

"Say mai-tai," Anne called out, snapping the picture just as Loni obeyed.

"Lovely," Anne said as she slipped the cover over the lens.

"Let's not stand out here wasting time," the woman who'd been introduced to Anne as Mama Chloe urged in a musical voice. "Come on up to the house. We have coffee and cake." She took Anne's elbow and steered her toward the steps.

"I hope I'm not putting you out," Anne murmured politely, returning the woman's infectious smile.

"Lordy, no. 'Sides, Quinn's never brought a lady here before, so you must be special to him, and that makes you special to us, too."

"I...thank you." Anne wondered if Quinn had

heard Mama Chloe's words and couldn't help turning around to catch his reaction.

If he'd heard, he gave no sign. He was now surrounded by the children of the family, all talking at once. Two of the tallest boys were trying to wrestle him to the ground, while a shy little girl hung on to his hand.

For a split second, when he looked up and their eyes met, she saw that he was laughing, his face relaxed, his eyes unguarded. She saw sweetness there and an innate gentleness, the kind only a strong man can possess.

She smiled, but her lips trembled as she raised her camera and snapped a shot. The laughter in his eyes faded, and a look like frustration hardened his mouth.

Anne felt as though the sun had dipped behind a cloud, even though it was still blazing brightly over the clearing.

"I don't know why Quinn changed his mind about coming for the party, but I'm glad he did." Anne turned to see Mama Chloe watching her, a smile curving her lips. "And brought you along."

Anne's grin faltered. "Changed his mind?" she echoed. "I don't understand."

"Never mind. I'm sure he had his reasons. Quinn never does anything without a reason."

Chapter Six

The luau began at sundown in a quiet, secluded grotto a half mile from the house. The setting recalled the celebrations of earlier times, before American missionaries changed island life forever.

Burning torches turned the twilight into golden daylight. Mats of pandanus leaves served as a table and chairs. The traditional poi and other staples were served in wooden calabashes and on platters.

Coconut milk for the children and a home brew made of fermented taro root known affectionately as *okolehoa* were served in coconut halves. Banana leaves served as plates. Men, women and children ate with their fingers.

Anne had never seen so many exotic dishes—pineapple brought first to the island by Captain Cook in the eighteenth century, wild bananas native to the islands and the large, juicy mangoes she had come to crave.

In the place of honor sat an enormous wooden platter containing the pig that had been roasting all day in a pit lined with banana leaves. The tail was a black corkscrew curl. The crusty brown face seemed to be smiling at her.

With the exception of the modern clothing, the only intrusions into the nineteenth-century atmosphere were Anne's camera and the wristwatches worn by most of the guests.

As the guests of honor, Loni was sitting at one end

of the long mat, her husband-to-be, Cully, at the other. Anne was sitting cross-legged near the middle. Mama Chloe sat to her right, occasionally translating the names of some of the dishes she passed to Anne. Quinn was on her left, stretched out full-length, his head propped on his hand.

Torchlight streaked his hair with the same golden hue as the sun-bleached hair on his arms. He seemed to be enjoying himself, although Anne noticed that he was drinking milk instead of the potent home brew, and that he ate very little.

After the first few courses and her first tentative sips of *okolehoa,* Anne began to relax and enjoy herself. At first the island liquor had tasted like sour apple juice and been difficult to swallow without grimacing. Now, she realized, she was beginning to like the tartness. Certainly it was going down much more easily.

Definitely delicious, she thought, as she raised the Nikon and framed Loni's face in the viewfinder. The girl was dressed in a white muumuu, and flowers were entwined in her dark hair. The happiness on her face gave her a radiance Anne envied.

"Take one of Cully before the *okolehoa* makes his mouth too numb to smile," Loni requested, beaming at her groom.

Anne had liked Cully Hayward on sight. He was only an inch or so taller than his bride, with thinning sandy hair and a face only his mother or a woman in love could call handsome. But his smile was engaging, and his compact body radiated masculine sex appeal.

Dark eyes gleaming, the groom raised his coconut shell, grinned, then downed half the contents in one swallow. The guests hooted and applauded as Anne captured his triumphant expression.

Nice people, she thought, smiling to herself. Happy. Friendly. Had Quinn been like that as a boy? she wondered. Had his dark eyes flashed with humor instead of pain? Had he laughed easily?

Her thoughts directed her gaze to his face. He was watching her impassively.

"Something wrong?" he asked in a voice too low to intrude into the general conversation.

"You're not drinking," she whispered. "Isn't that against the rules?"

One side of his mouth slanted. "I have my own rules."

"Me too," she said, taking another long swallow. "Mine say that all rules are off during wedding luaus."

Across from her, Loni's older brother, Tino, produced a ukulele and began to tune the strings. Someone else began strumming a guitar. Soon everyone was singing, the words melodious and oddly sad. Anne closed her eyes and let the music flow over her.

More alert than he wanted Anne to know, Quinn scanned the area, looking for signs of trouble. No one had followed them. He'd made certain of that. But that didn't mean they were safe.

He'd known men with uncanny tracking skills. Men with almost supernatural abilities to find the enemy. He'd been one of those men himself once, a long time ago. Too long ago.

His combat skills were rusty; his emotional edge had been blunted by his years on the ranch. He could handle dying alone. He couldn't handle watching Anne die.

Completing his visual check, he allowed his gaze to linger on Anne's face. The flickering torchlight brought out flaws—the faint shadows under her eyes, a chin that was too square, a mouth that was too generous for the fragile bone structure.

And yet she was so lovely, so utterly feminine, that it took his breath away to look at her. He wanted to bury himself and the regrets that tormented him inside her softness. He wanted to forget all the reasons why that would be a mistake.

"Quinn?"

His gaze searched her face before settling on the soft mouth so close to his. "What?"

"Can I ask you something?"

Her breath carried the same tangy scent as the numbing liquor he had denied himself. The hunger in him grew, clawing deep. "Why do I think I'm not going to like this?" he muttered, but his tone was indulgent.

She shook her coconut shell and gave him a hopeful look. "I'd like a teensy bit more, please," she murmured, sliding her tongue between her lips.

One dark eyebrow rose, and his mouth twitched. "If you have any more *okolehoa,* you won't be able to focus your eyes, let alone that camera you love so much."

Swaying to the music, Anne squinted at the nearest torch. The flame flickered sensuously. When one flame became two she would quit, she promised herself as she waved her coconut under his nose. "I've had stronger," she murmured over the slow, sultry throb of the music.

"Have you?"

"Hmm. In Brazil I drank goat's blood. Tasted awful, but the Indians who were my hosts were so sweet to me I didn't want to offend them, so I drank it all. 'Course, I was pretty sick for a while.''

"Don't say I didn't warn you," he said as he sat up and reached for the nearest gourd. He filled the coconut half-full and corked the gourd.

"Don't be so stingy," she murmured.

Quinn shook his head and poured more. "You are one stubborn lady, Anne Oliver," he muttered. "Too stubborn for your own good."

Watching intently, Anne noticed that his eyes were crinkling at the corners. When he wanted, he could be a very charming man. Too charming, she realized, taking a quick sip.

"And you're not, Quinn Sinclair?"

He turned his head slightly, and the torchlight played over his mouth. His hard, unyielding mouth. The mouth that had plundered hers.

"I learned a long time ago that the pleasure isn't always worth the pain. Seems you haven't learned that yet."

Anne drank deeply from the coconut, then licked the last drops from her lips. "But isn't that my choice?"

"Yes. As long as you know the risks you're taking." He got to his feet and extended his hand. "Time to turn in."

Mama Chloe turned her gaze from the musicians and uttered a cry of protest. "You two can't leave yet. It's time to begin the dancing."

For some reason Anne had a feeling Quinn knew that already. Didn't he want her to watch?

"We'll pass. Anne's had a long day, and—"

"No, I haven't," Anne put in. She swung her gaze

from Mama Chloe to Quinn. "I'm having so much fun, and I don't want to miss the dancing. You said there would be dancing."

"You make it hard for a man to take care of you." There was an edge to his voice, but he resumed his place next to her.

Mama's words had released a murmur of anticipation. Three of the men stood and disappeared into the thick tangle of ferns to the right.

Two others left the circle, only to return almost immediately carrying a variety of drums. Some were made of scooped-out logs with what looked like sharkskin stretched over the top. Others had been fashioned from large gourds.

Two of the women settled drums in front of them. A third took two of the gourds from one of the men. Anne heard a rattling sound as the woman returned to her place.

"What are those?" she asked Quinn.

"*Uliuli.* The Polynesian version of castanets."

At a gesture from Mama, the drumming began. Rhythmic, throbbing, intoxicating. Anne felt her heart beating faster, echoing the pounding urgency of the beat.

The same urgency built inside her until she was breathing faster and faster. And then, from the darkness, three figures leapt into the circle of the flares.

Nearly naked, their bodies gleamed in the firelight. A cloth of tapa bound their loins in the traditional way. Bracelets of boar tusks encircled their upper arms. Rattles of dog fangs jangled on their ankles.

The quick, menacing moves and the frantic thudding of the drums indicated a war dance. Anne had read enough to know that the dance was symbolic—

simulated spear thrusts that ended a hair's breadth from an unprotected chest, deadly kicks and chops of the hand that would have killed if they'd connected. Even so, the power of the mock battle was enormous.

Anne found that she was holding her breath, and she let it out slowly. She longed to capture this moment on film, but that might break the spell for the others.

Instead she contented herself with leaning forward to get closer. To absorb every nuance of the ancient movements. To draw the pounding rhythm inside her until she felt a part of the dancers.

Gradually she became aware of a change. The tempo slowed. The movements became more graceful. The drums were muted. Sharp, staccato steps became flowing. Arm and hand movements spoke of wooing instead of war. Graceful gestures promising rapture instead of death.

Lean male hips swayed suggestively. Provocatively. Tension stretched inside her, the same hard, painful tension that tightened Quinn's face.

His gaze met hers. Hot, dark need blazed in his. In hers, too? she wondered, looking away quickly.

One of the men held out a hand to a young woman who immediately rose and joined him, matching her movements to his. The second chose, and the twosomes began to dance. And then the third man came toward Anne, his hand extended, palm up.

Enthralled, Anne placed her hand in his and let herself be pulled to her feet. The lights became a blur. The music was inside her, compelling her to move.

Freedom, she thought. That was what the ancients had. Uninhibited, joyous freedom to express their emotions. Eyes half-closed, she whirled faster and faster, her heart racing, her blood surging.

In her mind it was Quinn who was dancing with her. Quinn's wooing that was exciting her. Quinn's spirit that was reaching out to her.

Anne stumbled. A strong hand held her until she caught her balance. Dazed, she glanced up, intending to murmur her thanks.

Her breath caught. For an instant she wondered if she was drunk. Were those truly Quinn's eyes she saw blazing with longing, Quinn's hand holding her, Quinn's mouth descending toward hers?

She swayed, and her hands clutched at his shirt. Through the material, she felt the heat of his body and the pounding of his heart.

With a harsh groan, he lifted her into his arms and walked out of the intimate circle of light and into the darkness. Anne pressed her face to his neck and inhaled the musky man-scent of his skin. Anger radiated from him, along with something more. Something as elemental and powerful as the dancing. Sexual hunger as urgent as the long strides taking them farther and farther from the others.

Lulled by the motion of his body, she was nearly asleep when, suddenly, she felt herself falling. She cried out, opening her eyes at the same time. She had a split-second image of a dimly lit room before she sprawled on her back against something soft. A bed.

Looking up, she saw a thatched roof, steeply sloped. Just as Quinn had promised, she was in one of the huts designed as future quarters for the tourists Mama hoped to attract.

Quinn was standing by the bed. His arms were folded. This time she had no trouble determining the color of his eyes. They were as black as the sky over-head, lit from within by a powerful emotion, held at bay by the control she had come to expect from him.

"You're angry with me," she murmured, defiantly meeting those dark eyes.

"Am I?"

"Is it because I was dancing?"

"What do you think?"

Anne sat up. "I think I'm having a wonderful time tonight."

Her hair tumbled over her shoulders, silky and thick. Her cheeks were pink, and her eyes were glow-ing. Her mouth, free of lipstick now, looked almost too tempting to resist.

Quinn felt the air grow thick. Suffocatingly thick, the way it was underwater when his air supply was nearly gone.

"Go to sleep, Anne. It's late."

She looked to one side, then to the other. There was only one bed in the room. "Where will you sleep?"

"On the floor," he said in an even tone.

"Why?"

"You're not in any shape to make decisions we both might regret," he said in that low, even tone. His gaze slid up the tense line of her neck to her face. Lingered. In the half-light, the angular lines of his lean face seemed too powerful, too compelling.

Anne sensed that the lack of emotion in his voice was deceptive. Instinct told her that Quinn was very much like the volcanoes that had created the islands, with crusts as hard and cold as dead ash on the out-side, seething with explosive power within.

"I was thinking of you," she murmured. "When I was dancing. I want you to make love to me."

Quinn sat down on the bed and tried to steady his pulse. His throat was dry, and his blood seethed.

"I can only give you tonight. No promises of tomorrow. No strings."

"I'm not asking for promises," she said softly. "Only tonight."

His breath came out in a shudder. "I'll make sure you don't get pregnant." His voice had a rusty quality. Painful memories? she wondered.

Her mouth went dry. "It's all right. I'm on the pill. Because of my...schedule. Traveling and all." To places where feminine hygiene wasn't even a concept.

Before she'd met Quinn, having to take that little pill every morning had been a nuisance. Now she was grateful her gynecologist had insisted.

One by one she undid the buttons of his shirt, then slipped her hands inside and flattened her fingers against his skin. It was smooth and warm, inviting a slow exploration.

Quinn watched her pupils grow wide and heard her breath catch. The warmth of her breath on his face sent pulses of hard need shooting deep. He felt his blood hammer in his head and pool in his groin.

"You can trust me, Quinn," she murmured, touching the tense line of his jaw with fingertips that trembled slightly. "I won't hurt you."

Quinn heard the gentleness in her husky voice. A hot urgency licked at his belly, and his breath suddenly felt too explosive for his lungs to hold. Slowly he lifted her fingers to his mouth. He kissed the tips. Her palm. The pulse throbbing at her wrist. Then he pushed her hand above her head and held it there.

"Hold me," she whispered as her fingers slowly caressed his massive shoulders. "Keep the nightmare away again."

His skin rippled in reaction, and the hard muscles beneath contracted. Above the intensity of his dark eyes, his eyebrows drew together as though he was feeling a sudden pain.

"It's been a long time. I don't want to hurt you." He flattened all emotion from his voice, but she heard the yearning buried there.

"You won't. I trust you."

"Tonight we both trust," he murmured on a rasping breath. Slowly he grasped the hand still clinging to his shoulder and pushed it over her head to join her other hand. She was completely helpless now. Vulnerable. Trapped.

He brought his head down slowly, and she found that she was holding her breath. His mouth brushed her throat, exploding the breath from her in a helpless rush.

"Sweet," he murmured before sliding his mouth to the tender skin below her ear. Then he let his tongue explore her ear, flicking in and out of the sensitive whorls.

He flattened her palms with his, then entwined their fingers. Anne turned toward his exploring mouth, impatient to feel those hard lips tasting hers. She lifted one leg and tried to twist toward him, but his heavy thigh captured hers, holding her.

He drew back, struggling to hang on to his concentration. To his control. Desire spiked hot and heavy between his thighs, urging him to drive deep into her soft, pliant body.

Her face was flushed, her eyes glittering with the

same desperate need to touch and be touched that was surging in him like adrenaline.

His mouth firmed over hers, firing a hungry response from her lips, which surprised him into a harsh groan. His hands grew possessive, sliding over the fragile bones of her throat to her shoulders, then her breasts.

Anne gasped as his fingers kneaded her already hardened nipples, exciting sensations of both pain and pleasure. Pain, because it had been so long since she had been touched so intimately; pleasure, because his touch was achingly gentle, almost adoring.

"Yes, oh, yes!" she cried against his hard, hungry mouth.

In answer his tongue plunged deep, rasping hot against hers. Quinn sensed the wildness that lay waiting just beyond the boundaries of her control. His own control threatened to shatter with each kiss, each soft moan his mouth was drawing from her.

"Patience," he managed to say between gentle, wooing kisses. "Or this will be over before we've started."

Anne heard the strain in his voice and smiled, even as she moaned in protest.

Because every nerve ending in his body was driving him to haste, he forced himself to undress her slowly, savoring the feel of her soft skin beneath his palms as he drew off her shirt. Her bra was silk and lace, utterly feminine and seductive. She moaned as his hands slipped it from her. Her breasts were luminous in the dim light and tipped with dark nipples.

Quinn's mouth replaced his hands, his tongue as deliciously caressing as his fingertips had been. Anne writhed, her hands eager, stroking down the corded length of his belly, tangling in the arrow of silky hair.

Her nails rasped against denim. Her fingers pushed beneath the constriction, and he gasped, his breath warming the moist cleft between her breasts.

Suddenly he rolled away, his breathing harsh and ragged. He stood and yanked down the tight jeans. Her own breathing rapid and shallow, Anne sat up and eased out of her slacks.

Her hands were on the elastic of her panties when he stopped her. "Let me," he whispered harshly. "I want to see all of you."

He kissed the curve of her belly, then slid the silky panties from her. Anne shivered and reached for him.

The bed dipped under his weight, and then she was enfolded in heat again. Heat from his body. Heat from hers. His leg slid between hers, rough where the hair curled dark against his bronzed skin, hardened by lean muscle and sinew.

His hands roamed over her, his fingers finding sensitive places that were as new to her as they were to him. Flashes of desire burned over her skin where his mouth and hands had prepared her.

Quinn felt the tremors running along her thighs where his hands stroked. His fingers suddenly trembled as they slipped inside her. She was warm silk, moist, ready.

Need clawed at him, more powerful than the hottest rage, more engulfing than the most potent bitterness. Feelings he had ruthlessly deadened for years threatened to erupt. Protective feelings. Tender feelings. Feelings too dangerous to be acknowledged.

With a groan that felt torn from him, he moved over her, his patience gone. He entered her slowly.

The cords on his neck were distended with the effort he was expending to keep his cries of pleasure locked inside.

Anne clung to him, her legs wide, her body opening willingly to admit his. Pleasure spiraled inside her like a vortex, whirling faster and faster until she was consumed, her cries mindless, ecstatic.

Her nails raked his back, urging him to move. His first gentle movements released the last of her will. She gave herself over to him, her heat mingling with his, her body melting into his.

She opened her eyes, needing to see his face. His eyes were closed, the thick black lashes quivering slightly against the hard planes of his cheeks.

His skin glistened with dampness. His breathing was labored, the sounds of pain and pleasure mingling as though torn from his deep chest.

She moaned, trying to match him thrust for thrust. And then the vortex within her was out of control, spinning, spinning, until she was a part of it. Mindless, breathless, her pleasure was a long-drawn-out cry that Quinn caught in his mouth.

His body convulsed, the muscles bunching and straining against her skin. She thought he cried her name, but the waves of pleasure taking her made it difficult to know for sure.

And then she was falling, drifting in warmth, Quinn's head cradled against her breasts, their bodies joined.

Her fingers stroked his thick, soft hair. In the muted light, it seemed as black as the moonless sky, but, like the Hawaiian night, the strands felt warm against her fingers.

She sighed with the pleasure of the afterglow, filling her with a serenity she hadn't felt in a long time. Violence and hate and fear seemed far away. No one could find her when she was cradled in Quinn's strong arms. Nothing could hurt her while he was with her.

"Mmm, lovely," she murmured.

She felt the muscles of his cheek tighten against her breast and thought he must be smiling. He wasn't. In fact, when he raised his head to look at her, his mouth was hard with tension. "Did I hurt you?"

"No, of course not," she murmured, running her fingers over the forceful line of his mouth. Her body tingled in private places, wonderful places.

"No regrets?"

He let his fingers gently push through the thick, pale curls framing her face, until the softness brushed his wrists. Beneath the rough pads of his thumbs, he felt the blood throbbing in the veins beneath her satiny skin.

"No, no regrets. You're a very generous man, when you let yourself be."

His hands clenched in the rumpled silk of her hair, the only part of him that moved. "No," he said, his voice dull. "I'm not."

She smiled; the feel of his mouth was still imprinted on her lips. "You're really a lot gentler than you want people to know," she said, turning to kiss the strong wrist so close to her cheek.

His pulse leapt. "Anne, there's nothing in me that you would want. I wish there was."

"I'm not so sure. I think there's more in you than you know. Good things. Things to be proud of."

His mouth compressed. "You're crazy, that's what

you are." An emotion he couldn't define thickened his voice and tightened his gut.

She laughed, feeling wonderful. "No, I'm just happy. Life is very good when the nightmares stay away."

Quinn thought about the men of the Aryan American Brigade who even now might be trying to find her. To kill her. His Anne.

Rage spiked with frustration twisted in his gut. The bastards would never get her. Not while he was alive.

He turned onto his side and settled her against him. "Go to sleep, *ipo*," he murmured.

Anne snuggled against him, her mind running through the Hawaiian phrases in her guidebook. Sweetheart, she thought. He'd called her sweetheart.

Anne woke to an unfamiliar quiet. She was marvelously relaxed, even though her body ached in private, intimate ways that brought a warm rush of pleasure to her face.

Dawn was hovering, casting just enough light into the hut to show her that Quinn was still asleep. He was sprawled on his back. One hand was tucked under his pillow. The other was curled over her thigh, as though, in his sleep, he needed to be connected to her.

His big chest rose and fell easily, and his breathing was steady. The sheet was bunched between them, covering her but not him.

In sleep, his body was totally vulnerable. And yet, the long, muscled length of him suggested power and strength. He was partly aroused, as though he were replaying their lovemaking in his dreams.

She lay perfectly still, studying the deeply etched

tension that never left his face, even in sleep. His jaw was dark with whisker stubble. His brow was scored with faint lines that never disappeared. Unlike her, he had no scars on his body. No obvious marks of suffering. But they were there, inside, where healing was the most difficult.

It made her sad to imagine what life must be like for him. The loneliness he had condemned himself to endure. The bitterness that ate at him.

From somewhere close she heard the mournful call of a dove. It was a lonely sound. An answering sigh eased from her lips.

Today they would attend Loni's wedding. Together they would toast the young couple's happiness. Perhaps they would spend one more night alone—here, where the world seemed far away.

And then what?

As though hearing her question, Quinn frowned and muttered something in his sleep. His brows drew together, and a long, heavy breath like a groan escaped his parted lips.

Anne wanted to kiss away the demons that were disturbing his sleep, but she felt suddenly shy. In many ways he was a stranger, this man who had discovered depths of passion in her that she hadn't even dreamed existed.

He knew her body, but he didn't know her. To him, she was a rich, snooty fashion model like his ex-wife. Anne shook with a sudden chill. She had asked him to trust her. Would he feel used when he discovered she had been lying to him?

A woman's lie had nearly destroyed him once. She didn't want him to be hurt again.

Franklyn was wrong. Quinn did need to know the

truth about her, and he needed to know now. As soon as he awoke, she would tell him.

Flattening her hand against the cool sheet, she slid her fingers under the pillow, searching for his strong, warm hand. She needed to touch him. To feel the life in his skin and the security of his strength next to her.

But instead of his hand, she touched something cold and hard. Frowning, she pulled it out from under the pillow.

It was a pistol. A big, ugly, deadly revolver. And it was loaded.

Chapter Seven

Fear ignited in her stomach, making her queasy. Scarcely daring to breathe, she eased to a sitting position and clutched the sheet to her breast. Awkwardly, using her free hand, she wrapped the sheet around her. Her other hand tightened around the grip made for a bigger hand than hers.

She took a deep breath. Calm down, Annie. Lots of men carry guns. For…for snakes and things. Except there were no snakes in Hawaii. No predatory animals running wild. No real dangers at all. Except for the human kind.

She cleared her throat. "Quinn? Quinn, wake up."

His lashes fluttered, then lifted. She saw a smile in his eyes—until he noticed the gun barrel pointed at his chest.

His face went still. His gaze remained riveted on the pistol. "Anne, that trigger has a very light pull."

"Something tells me this isn't a wedding gift."

"No."

The pistol was surprisingly heavy. But then, the bullets were lead, weren't they? And there were six of them in the cylinder. She wet her suddenly dry lips.

"Do you always travel with a gun?"

"Not exactly." Quinn watched her, trying to decide how to handle her. He wasn't kidding about the pull on the trigger. A mere twitch would be enough to blow a hole in his chest the size of his fist.

"Exactly what *is* it doing under your pillow, then?"

"Give it to me first and I'll tell you."

Anne shook her head. "Not until you explain why you brought it."

Quinn tightened the muscles of his spine and legs, but he made himself lie motionless. "Anne, I know about the Brigade. And I know why you're in the Witness Protection Program."

Anne gaped at him, growing colder and colder. The gun barrel wavered. "How do you know?"

"Ed Franklyn told me."

She paled. Suspicion clouded her eyes. "I don't believe you. He wouldn't. Not when he made me promise not to say a word."

"Call him."

Doubt flickered across her face. "There's no phone here."

"We'll go up to the house. Mama Chloe has a phone." Mama Chloe's house was on the other side of the clearing, beyond the grotto where the luau had been held.

Anne searched his face. She saw tension there. And a steady, patient look in his eyes. But his mouth was set. His body had a stillness that was chilling.

"Okay, but I'll get dressed first. Don't move till I tell you to." Her clothes were scattered over the floor where Quinn had thrown them. His were there, too. Mixed with hers.

Still holding the gun steady with one hand, she managed to get to her knees and clutch the sheet to her breasts. Quinn's expression didn't change. Still, she had never felt so vulnerable, so exposed.

Awkwardly, she crawled backward. Her foot tangled in a fold of the sheet, tipping her sideways. Quinn moved so quickly that she had no time to cry out before his powerful fingers clamped around her wrist.

He pushed her arm upward just as her finger instinctively tightened. The gun went off with an explosive force that drove her backward and made her ears ring.

His curse was equally explosive. Pain shot through her wrist as Quinn wrested the gun from her and thumbed on the safety.

"You could have killed both of us!" she shouted, rising to her knees again and facing him. She forgot, for the moment, that she had lost the protective covering of the sheet.

"Me?" he shouted. "Are you crazy, woman? I wasn't the one waving the damn gun around."

"You should have known how I'd react if I saw it! You could have told me."

"I had a reason—"

Suddenly he heard a sound that froze the rest of his explanation. Chopper blades. High-pitched, like a gunship, coming in fast and low.

"Get dressed," he ordered, giving her a shove before he vaulted from the big old-fashioned bed and snatched up his jeans.

Anne watched with a stunned expression. "What?"

"Hear that?" he asked, nodding in the direction of the sound that was rapidly growing louder. "Might be friendly, might not be. I'm not taking any chances until I know one way or the other."

Still holding his revolver in one hand, Quinn shoved his legs into his jeans and jerked them over his thighs. He had fastened enough of the metal buttons to anchor the soft denim to his hips and was already heading for the door when Anne scrambled off the bed.

The mattress was higher than normal, causing her to lose her balance and stumble against the nightstand. By the time she had regained her balance, Quinn had the door open and was searching the sky through the thick tangle of tree branches overhead.

"Be careful," she shouted, but he was already pulling the door shut behind him.

"Oh, God," she muttered. "If he gets himself killed…"

Biting her lip, she snatched clean underwear from the saddlebags and dressed as quickly as her shaking hands would permit. She was shoving her feet into her boots when the door slammed open and Quinn burst through at a dead run.

"Get down!" he shouted, even as he dove forward. His body crashed into hers, and they sprawled to the floor, his chest crushing her breasts and driving the air from her lungs.

Through a gasp of pain and outrage, she heard a roar overhead. Noise pounded her eardrums and made her teeth rattle. The floorboards vibrated, and the windows shook.

In one violent motion Quinn wrapped his arms around her and rolled them both under the bed. At the same moment bullets strafed the hut.

Lead slugs thudded into the double layer of mattress and box springs above them and ripped into the floor as though it were canvas, leaving a trail of holes like stitches. Bits of thatch and splintered wood rained down. Glass shattered, shards exploding inward.

Anne tried to scream, but she found she couldn't draw breath. Her lungs burned. Her body shook. Her fingers clutched Quinn's shirt. Just when she knew she was going to die, the roar began to fade. Anne inhaled deeply, greedy for air. Still gripped by terror, she was afraid to move.

"Are you all right?" Quinn asked, his breath warm and reassuring against her neck.

She nodded, and his arms tightened. "Is...is it gone?" she whispered when her throat relaxed enough to allow speech.

Quinn raised his head and listened. "Sounds like it. Better give it a few more seconds to make sure."

"Thank God," she murmured, closing her eyes.

God had nothing to do with it, Quinn thought with a private, cynical smile. God was never there when you needed Him.

"It's the Brigade, isn't it?" she asked against the comfort of his warm neck.

"Looks that way. Probably tracked us from the ranch, then radioed for the chopper." He bit off a curse. "I blew it, Anne. I had intended to scout around last night after the luau, but I...fell asleep."

"You expected them?" she cried.

"I...knew it was a possibility, yes."

"How did you know?"

"Eddie called."

"When?"

Quinn hesitated. She was withdrawing from him. He could feel it. "Yesterday morning. Early."

Anne let go of him, her hands shaking. "That's why you brought me here, isn't it? To protect me. Not because you wanted my company. The sex was just a bonus."

Quinn's eyes flashed dangerously. "You know better than that."

"Do I?" Her voice was thick and wavering. Quinn sensed the hurt shimmering beneath the anger. It was better that way, he told himself, even as he fought a need to kiss the pain from her eyes.

"I told you where I stand, Anne. The choice was yours." He rolled free and stood up. The room was ruined. Furniture splintered. Walls blasted. The mattress that had saved their lives pockmarked.

Outside, a pair of roof-high palm trees had been chopped in two by the hail of high-powered machine-gun shells. The surrounding ferns had been shredded like paper. The air smelled dusty.

Anne eased out from under the bed and sat up. Her stomach was jumping uncontrollably, and her mouth was so dry it was hard to swallow.

"That was close," she said with a shudder she couldn't quite master. She rested her back against the bed and tried to ignore the spinning in her head.

"Close enough." He snatched up his shirt and shrugged into it. "We got lucky."

"They'll be back, won't they?"

Quinn passed a critical eye over her face. Her lips were white, her skin so pale it seemed translucent. Her hair was a tumble of curls. She looked shaken, but controlled. He hoped that she was tough enough to take the truth. If she wasn't, they were both in trouble.

"Right now, the bastards are probably landing about six miles from here in a meadow near Cook's Ridge. If they're as good as I think they are, they'll double-time back here to make sure we're dead.

We've got an hour, maybe less, to get as far away from here as we can.''

"What...what about Mama Chloe? Oh, God, Quinn, what about Loni? We have to warn them. To...to do something.'' Anne scrambled to her feet and started toward the door. Quinn hauled her back.

"Easy, honey,'' he ordered, his fingers restraining her.

Anne struggled to free herself. She had to warn them. "Let me go! I can't let it happen again. I can't...''

Quinn pulled her hard against him and wrapped his arms around her. Her body shook against his. "These men are pros, Anne. They have a job to do—kill a potential threat to their leader. Anything else isn't part of their mission.''

"But—''

"As long as we stay away from the house and the others, they'll be safe.''

Anne stared up at him, her heart racing. "This... this is just like my nightmare. I...can't wait until I wake up.''

One side of his mouth saluted her try at levity. Under the stubble, his jaw was set. "Me, too.''

His mouth came down on hers. His kiss was demanding, bordering on desperate. His arms wrapped tighter, pulling her hard against him. She dug her fingers into his shoulders, trying to get closer. Her mouth moved under his, answering his demand with one of her own. She felt herself begin to tremble. From need this time.

Quinn felt the small tremors take her body. His own was none too steady. He knew that they needed to leave. He knew that the hunger that surged in him couldn't be satisfied.

He deepened the kiss. His breath rasped against hers. His thighs rubbed hers. His hands roamed greedily.

The promises he wanted to make and couldn't, the words she deserved that weren't in him to say, the longings he was too proud to express—those things he put into his kiss.

Quinn was breathing hard when he finally managed to relax his grip on her. He waited for her to open her eyes. When she did, he saw that she was as aroused as he was. Her lips parted, still rosy from the pressure of his, and she smiled.

"Think you can ride now? There's a village a long day's ride south of here, with a sheriff's substation. We'll head there."

Anne managed a shaky nod. "Much as I'm enjoying myself, I guess we'd better go."

Silently, his hand in hers, he led her to the dresser. Still without speaking, he looped her camera over her neck, grabbed the saddlebags she had hastily packed and led the way to the door.

Neither looked back.

"I used to love the rain," Anne said with a deep sigh. "But that was when I was curled up with a good book in front of a roaring fire, eating warm brownies and drinking cold milk."

Resting her elbows on her crossed knees, she watched a steady drizzle pelt a bush that had large leaves shaped like elephant ears.

"Me, I'd rather have brandy and a cigar," Quinn said without opening his eyes.

"Right now that sounds wonderful, even the cigar," she muttered, wiggling her toes. Her boots were soaked; miraculously, her socks were dry.

The shelter where she and Quinn had taken refuge was enclosed on three sides by walls of lava rock a yard thick. The roof sloped downward from a height of ten feet or so to the entrance, where it was only a few inches above Quinn's head, giving the small area a cavelike feeling. Unlike a cave, however, the floor where they had spread their saddle blankets was man-made of flat lava stones, laid close together like tiles.

Crude though it might be, it kept them dry and relatively warm. Oblivious to the steady downpour, the horses grazed nearby, hobbled to prevent them from straying too far.

It was late afternoon. How late, Anne could only guess. She hadn't seen the sun since midmorning, and her watch had been smashed when Quinn had thrown her to the floor.

The rain had started several hours after they'd ridden away from the ruined hut, heading south along a narrow, twisting trail. Unlike most of the afternoon showers Anne had become accustomed to, this one showed no sign of stopping.

By the time Quinn had indicated that they were to stop, she had been shivering and miserable. A change of clothes had warmed her skin, and she'd used her discarded shirt to dry her hair. But she couldn't do anything about the empty feeling in the pit of her stomach.

"Is this what you call a monsoon?" she asked, propping her chin on the heel of her palm.

Quinn opened one eye and inspected the sheet of water cascading over the eaves like a waterfall. He was sitting a few feet away with his back against his worn saddle, one leg drawn up at the knee. The stubble on his jaw had darkened, giving him a slightly disreputable appearance that Anne liked.

"If this was summer, yeah," he said finally. "Now I call it a damned nuisance."

Anne heard the irritation in his voice and thought about the apple they had shared at noon. It was all either of them had eaten. She was hungry, but a man of his size had to be ravenous.

"Are you sure it's safe? To stop, I mean?" she asked.

"Safe or not, we don't have much choice. The trail thins out about a mile south, and then it's straight down. It's too risky for the horses in the mud."

"If it's risky for the horses, it has to be risky for...anyone following us, right?"

"Depends."

"On what?"

"On how they're following. If it was me, I'd get a fix on the subject's direction, then search the area by chopper."

"Subject," she echoed. "Is that what I am?"

Quinn sat up and flexed the tired muscles of his back. "To them, yes."

Anne glanced at the sky. The clouds were so low they obliterated the tops of the tallest trees. Thank God it was rotten weather for flying. Or was it? She decided she didn't want to know.

"I've been a real problem for you, haven't I?" she said with a smile.

"Yes." The drawn, strained edges of his mouth told her more about his mood than the curt answer.

"I'm sorry."

"Don't be." He hesitated, then added in a rough tone, "For what it's worth, I think you're one brave lady. I wouldn't want to take on a bunch of goons with just a camera."

Surprised, Anne stared at him. Something in his eyes brought a strange flutter to her throat. She wanted to believe that it was love. She knew she didn't dare.

"Have you ever been afraid, Quinn?" she asked in a low tone. "Deep down in your soul scared?"

"Yes." His answer was gentle, encouraging her to continue.

"When?"

"On a dive in Australian waters when a twelve-foot great white was trying to decide whether or not to have me for dinner."

"What did you do?"

"Tried not to pee my pants and did my best to look unappetizing."

Anne laughed. "It must have worked."

"Guess it did." The lazy slur of amusement in his voice warmed her.

Anne got to her feet, too tense to sit any longer. She walked to the entrance and held out her hand.

The rain was cold. She waited until her cupped palm was full, then brought it to her mouth for a drink.

"It's good," she said. "Not as good as *okolehoa,* though." She looked over her shoulder and gave him a slightly abashed grin. "Now that was good! You should have had some."

"I've had my share."

Anne let her grin widen. "I'll just bet you have."

Watching her, Quinn wondered why he had

thought he could resist her. Why he had wanted to try.

He got to his feet and stretched, then joined her at the entrance. "Hell of a day for a wedding," he said.

Anne sobered. "I hope nothing's happened to your family."

His fingers rubbed the tender place in the middle of her back. "Strange as it sounds, guys like Draygon have a strange sense of honor."

While he'd been branded as dishonorable, Anne thought. She inhaled deeply, filling her lungs with the damp air. It smelled musty.

"What is this place, anyway?" she asked, needing to fill the silence.

"It's called a *puuhonua*. Roughly translated, it means sanctuary." His arm circled her shoulder, and she leaned into his hard, solid body.

"Like a church?"

"More like a refuge, although there was a priest here. In the old times, if you broke *kapu* by stepping on the chief's shadow or eating forbidden food, you were sentenced to death. By stoning, usually."

"Good Lord," Anne muttered. "I take it they didn't have much of a crime problem in those days?"

His laugh warmed her. "More than you'd think. But there was an appeal process, a sort of court of last resort."

"Even then?"

"Even then. If you made it here without being killed on the way, the priests would purify your soul, and you were forgiven. They also did the same for escaped prisoners of war or disgraced warriors."

"Just like that?"

"Just like that. Things were...simpler then." The

strange note in his voice drew her gaze. He was staring fixedly at the sodden walls enclosing the grassy area, and she knew he was thinking of his past.

"Is that why you came home?" she asked softly. "For refuge? After the court-martial?"

His gaze met hers. Held. Narrowed. His arm dropped from her shoulder, leaving her feeling cold and abandoned.

"Who told you?"

"Meg." He frowned and she hastened to add, "Don't be angry with her. She knew I wanted to understand you better. She thought knowing about your past might help."

"That sounds like Meg."

Once, she would have considered the hard slant of his smile cruel and unfeeling. Now that she knew him better, she sensed that his coldness was a defense against feelings so strong they had once nearly destroyed his life.

"You made a mistake, Quinn. It's a very human thing to do."

"Oh, I'm human, all right," he drawled, his mouth twisting. "When I'm around you, I'm very aware of just how human I am."

He moved closer. His hand tested a stray curl, rubbing the silky strands between his fingers. "You have a way of making a man want to take chances he shouldn't," he said, curling his hand around her neck.

He kissed her gently at first, but his restraint soon broke. His big hands roamed her back as though he was trying to memorize the soft curves and angles of the body pressed against his.

Anne stretched closer, her hands framing his face, her lips moving enticingly under his. This might be the last time they were together. The last time she could love him.

Taking his time, as though this was the most important task he had ever performed, he kissed her with slow, deep movements of his tongue.

His leg slid between hers until she rode his muscle-thick thigh. He moved slowly, sinuously, sending velvet spikes of pleasure thrusting into her with sweet insistence.

Quinn heard her small feminine moans of pleasure, and his body clenched at the feeling of savage possessiveness that ripped through him. Two centuries had passed since his people had been warriors, but the instinct to defend his *ohana,* his family, to the death still burned in him.

Anne was more than family. She was a part of him. His soul.

Quinn was breathing hard when he finally managed to relax his grip on her. He waited for her to open her eyes. When she did, he saw that she was as aroused as he was. Her lips parted, still rosy from the pressure of his.

The rain beat down steadily, forming a curtain enclosing them in the shelter. The air smelled fresh. Beyond the opening, the grass was a vivid green.

''Wow,'' she murmured, her voice thick.

''I'll say,'' he muttered, lowering his head again. It was like the first time, a gentle exploration that excited her as much as the fiercest demand. More.

She clung to his shoulders, the pounding of her heart almost as loud as the rain. Quinn knew that she was his—for the time left to them.

He forced patience into his hands as he worked at the buttons of her shirt. His knuckles moved against her skin. She inhaled in a rush, her eyes going very dark and turbulent.

"Hurry," she whispered, trying to help him with the last button.

"Not a chance. This has to last me a long time." He brushed kisses over her face before he pushed her shirt over her shoulders. It fluttered to the floor in a slither of soft cotton. Her bra was next.

The air was cool, making his hands seem wonderfully warm as they molded her breasts. It hurt to breathe. It hurt to wait. Her nipples swelled until they were hard and exquisitely sensitive.

Eagerly, impatiently, she leaned into his callused palms, rubbing against him. His chest lifted in a deep, shuddering breath.

And then he was stepping back to shuck off his own shirt, baring his wide, hairy chest. Anne leaned forward to kiss the hard, rounded cap of his shoulder. His muscles leapt under her lips, sending ripples over his skin.

Quinn pressed his lips together to stop the groan rising in him. He closed his eyes, enduring the wash of pleasure he was helpless to resist. All she had to do was touch him and he lost the iron discipline over his mind that had kept him strong. He hungered. He needed. The emotions were elemental, savage, not to be denied.

He lifted her into his arms and she curled against him, her arms around his neck. His mouth brushed hers over and over, his tongue darting between her lips to taste and tease.

When he could wait no longer, he took her to the floor and settled her gently on the saddle blanket. He pushed her backward, then unzipped her jeans and tugged them free to reveal a thin wedge of white satin curving high over her hips.

His hand cupped her intimately, causing her breath to catch. His hard fingers rubbed expertly, sending pleasure surging through her.

She moaned and arched against him. Her hand caught at his arm and she tried to pull him closer, moaning out her desperate need. His muscles contracted against her fingers, but he didn't give in to her demands. Instead he slipped a finger beneath the elastic to stroke and rub until she trembled.

Quinn was drunk on his need, his head swimming, his body swollen and hot behind the fly of his jeans. The pressure was excruciating. Yet he couldn't get enough of her. He took her nipple in his mouth and sucked.

She moaned, arching off the blanket in a spasm of need. His own need was clawing at him. Hands shaking, he drew back to struggle out of his boots and clothing.

Anne reached for him, her eyes dark and wild, her lips trembling. He came toward her quickly, his need now a savage, twisting demand.

Her body arched; her thighs opened. She reached for him, and he surrendered, thrusting deep and hard into her. Her body stretched to accept him, sending a shudder deep into him.

Sensations he had never felt before surged in his blood, like a fire out of control, eating at him, warming him. He kept his gaze on her face, hungry for the sight of her response.

Her cheeks were flushed, her lips parted and swollen, her lashes quivering on her cheeks. As he watched, her tongue licked across her lips, making his own mouth hungry again.

Anne's body was heavy, quivering. With each slow, shuddering thrust of his body, Quinn was releasing needs in her that she had ruthlessly denied, needs that now consumed her.

She cried out, her breathing rushed. Still he held back, needing to give her all that he had, all that he longed to be.

Sweat from his body and hers mingled. Skin slid against skin. He shuddered, struggling to hold back until she climaxed. And then they were both out of control.

Anne cried out, pleasure suffusing her. Quinn's cry was torn from him, exploding against her damp neck. And then they were spent, clinging together.

"Until you leave the island, you're my woman," he whispered, his smoldering gaze boring into hers. "I'll kill anyone who tries to hurt you."

"Yes," she murmured. "I'm your woman."

Careful to keep their bodies fused, Quinn rolled onto his back, cradling her against his warmth. She snuggled against him, her breath warming his neck, her softness like a drug.

As long as he held her, the dishonor and shame he'd lived with for so long seemed like a distant nightmare, no longer able to torment him. As long as he held her, he was at peace.

Chapter Eight

The deep pulse of high-speed rotors woke Quinn at first light. The chopper was heading northeast to southwest, flying a grid pattern, most likely. Methodically searching the area for two riders. Smart, he thought. Professional.

If the brush hadn't been so dense, Anne probably would have been dead by now. Him, too.

He'd heard the rain stop a few hours before dawn. If he'd been alone, he would have saddled Kanaloa and taken his chances. But he wasn't alone.

Slowly he turned to look at the woman using his shoulder for a pillow. She was wearing two of her shirts and one of his over her jeans. Her hair was disheveled, and her face was sunburned. In the rush to leave, her hat had been left behind, and she'd refused to wear his. They'd wasted ten minutes arguing—until he'd thrown up his hands in defeat.

Obstinate woman, he thought. More than obstinate. Bullheaded. A man would be hard pressed to hold his own against a woman like that. She would give as good as she got. Better, probably.

Emotions he hadn't known he still possessed ripped through him. Savage, primitive feelings he didn't dare name, feelings that were all too alive and twisting in his gut.

"Anne, wake up," he whispered against the tumble of her hair. "We have to go."

Anne sighed and stirred, still more asleep than

awake. The air touching her face carried a chill, but she was nestled against Quinn's warmth, covered by his shirt and protected by his arms. Her body was heady and relaxed. It was too much trouble to move.

"Anne?"

"Mmm?" Anne smiled, but refused to open her eyes.

His mouth brushed her smile, surprising her into looking at him. "Sun's coming up," he said, his voice oddly gruff.

"So I see." Ducking her head, she burrowed her fingers under the open collar of his shirt to find the soft hair on his chest and snuggled closer. Beneath her palm, his heart thudded erratically.

"It isn't good for a person to just leap out of bed first thing in the morning. Or, in this case, off this feather-soft saddle blanket you so cleverly provided for us." Her smile curved again, and her fingers worked at the buttons of his shirt.

Hunger splintered through him. "We at Sinclair Ranch aim to please, ma'am." He spoke lightly, but his body was surging to life under her touch.

His shirt was open now. And so was the top button of his jeans. Her fingers ran over the corrugated hardness of his ribs to find the soft whorl of hair surrounding his navel. He sucked in his breath, and the pounding of his heart reverberated through his chest.

Excitement welled in her. Quinn was as vulnerable to her as she was to him. More so, because he couldn't hide his response.

Her fingers dipped beneath the material of his jeans to tangle in hair that was coarser and tightly curled. This time his indrawn breath sounded like a groan.

"I have no complaints," she murmured. "Especially with the special attention from the owner."

"Is that right?"

"Mmm."

Her hand moved lower until she found his hot arousal. This time Quinn couldn't control the groan that shuddered through him. His hand trapped hers.

"Don't, baby," he grated, his voice harsh. "I'm in enough trouble as it is."

Anne laughed and rubbed her cheek against his shoulder. "No matter how you meant that remark, I intend to take it as a compliment," she murmured before trailing nibbling kisses along the slope of his shoulder to the warm hollow of his neck.

"Anne," he warned, but her mouth cut off his protest. She gave herself to him, trying to compress all the years they might have had into this moment. This instant.

Quinn was breathing hard when he finally managed to drag his mouth from hers.

"Time to get going." His voice was rough, made that way by his longing to make promises he couldn't keep.

Silently he rolled away and stood. He extended his hand and she took it. He pulled her to her feet, then bent to retrieve her camera and the saddlebags.

"Five minutes to use the facilities, primitive as they are," he said, looping her camera over her head and settling the worn leather strap against her neck. "I'll saddle the horses."

"I'll take care of Sadie. After all, this is the last day she'll be mine."

"Ed and his people should be at Hamakua by now. Once we get there you'll be safe."

''Yes, safe.''

He turned to look at her. His hand came up to gently brush the tangled hair away from her face. Her arms went around his neck, and she swayed toward him. Her mouth was only inches away from his.

An unexpected wave of tenderness nearly drove him to his knees. Through sheer force of will, he kept himself from pulling her into his arms again. ''Promise me you'll do exactly as I tell you,'' he said in a voice he couldn't quite sharpen into a command.

Anne let her fingers play in the unruly hair at the back of his neck. ''If you promise *me* that you won't take foolish chances. I love you, Quinn. I don't want you to die.''

He started to speak, but found that he couldn't. Instead he pressed his mouth to hers so gently she trembled.

''Don't look at me like that,'' she whispered. ''I didn't plan to fall in love. It just…happened.''

''God, I wish—''

Whatever he'd been going to say was cut off by the sudden rumble overhead. The helicopter was back.

Anne's head bobbed to her chest and she awoke with a start. Sadie tossed her mane, her gait slow and steady.

Anne straightened her spine, trying to work out the stiffness in her sore muscles. Her thighs ached, and her bottom felt numb.

Ahead, Quinn and his big bay seemed tireless. He sat in a comfortable slouch, his shoulders relaxed, his thighs fluid, as though the saddle was as comfortable as a favorite chair. The pistol rode high on his belt in a worn holster.

The helicopter was no longer overhead, allowing her to breathe easier. The trail was still treacherous, sloping downward at a frightening angle. A thick snarl of vines and bushes grew close on the left. On the right, much too near for her peace of mind, was a steep drop-off.

In the worst places Anne gave the mare her head, trusting the smart little pinto to keep her footing. But the trail was less than three feet wide in spots, bordered by loose rocks that added to the danger.

"Easy, girl," she murmured to the mare. "We're almost—"

"Son of a bitch!" Quinn reined in so violently that his mount reared. At the same time, he kicked his feet out of the stirrups and slid over the stallion's tail to the ground.

Sadie shied, and one of her hind legs slipped, but she managed to stay on the trail. "Quinn, what—?"

"Ambush!" he yelled as he slapped Kanaloa's rump. The stallion bolted, his ears laid back and his eyes rimmed with white.

Anne had already freed her feet from the stirrups when Quinn's arm encircled her waist and dragged her from the saddle. He shouted something. His hat went flying.

At the same moment Anne saw two men in camouflage, crouching at the edge of the trail, firing directly at her. Bullets kicked at the dirt close to the mare's hooves. Sadie whirled, sending loose rocks rolling down the hill, and took off the way they'd come.

Quinn gave Anne a shove into the thick brush.

Whiplike plants tore at her hair and lashed her face. She fell forward, but the thick mat of vegetation beneath her kept her from breaking an arm or leg.

Momentum sent them tumbling down the steep incline. Foliage closed in behind them. The world was a blur, going by at a sickening pace. She was helpless, as ungainly as a large rock caught in an avalanche, until finally she reached the bottom. Quinn's heavy body slammed against her, smashing her breasts into the ground.

They had landed in the deepest part of the gorge, where the vegetation was thickest. Everything was green, even the moss-covered stones.

Somewhere behind them bullets raked the underbrush. The noise was horrendous. And then—suddenly—silence.

Trapped under Quinn's weight, Anne couldn't move. Her breath was coming in gasps. Her elbow ached where she'd banged it on something. One palm was badly skinned. Her ankle felt bruised. The stench of rotting vegetation was overpowering.

"Have…they…gone?" she managed to grate out.

Quinn shifted his weight, and she was able to breath more deeply.

"No," he answered in a tone that was barely audible. "They're waiting for us to move."

Anne froze. "Are you all right?" she whispered.

"So far. How about you?"

Anne was so scared her mouth was sandpaper dry. "Still in one piece."

His gaze, narrowed now and so dark she saw nothing of the man who had made love to her, traveled swiftly over her.

"Bastards suckered me," he said, his voice very

quiet and made raspy by cold anger. "Probably spotted us early, figured out where we were heading, and then stayed away so we wouldn't change direction."

"How did they get here? I didn't see the helicopter anywhere."

"Either rappeled down from the chopper or came up the trail from below. There's a spot there where a gutsy pilot could land."

Anne bit her lip, trying not to show fear. Her elbow was beginning to ache badly, and her back was stiffening.

"Ms. Oliver? You still alive down there?" a rough male voice shouted from someplace above them.

Quinn stiffened. "Don't move," he mouthed.

"Come on out, Ms. Oliver." The shouted words seemed to reverberate through her head. "We won't hurt you. We just want to offer you a deal."

Quinn shook his head. Anne bit her lip and nodded that she understood.

"It's a good deal, Ms. Oliver," the voice wheedled. "You ought to think real hard before you turn it down."

Anne tried to control the frantic gallop of her pulse. Overhead, she heard a flutter of wings. Brush crackled under foot.

"The bastards are moving," Quinn told her. "Following the trail we made falling down this damn hill."

Suddenly the silence was shattered again by the earsplitting retorts of automatic rifle fire. Twenty feet above and to the left of their hiding place, lead slugs ricocheted off rocks and shredded the vegetation.

Quinn pulled her into his arms. She began to shake,

and her teeth started to chatter. A scream started someplace inside, but she forced it down.

"Easy, honey," Quinn whispered against her ear. She clung to him, pressing her face against the warm muskiness of his neck. They were going to die. Both of them.

The shooting stopped again without warning. The silence was worse, she decided as Quinn drew away from her.

Moving slowly, cautiously, he positioned himself so that he was on his knees with his head still covered by the green thatch of weeds.

Anne twisted into a more comfortable position, trying not to make a sound. Silence lay between them for several beats before Quinn brushed his thumb across a stinging place on her cheekbone.

"You're going to have a bad bruise," he whispered.

"Good thing I'm not really a model," she said with a smile that wobbled only slightly at the corners.

The flash of emotion in his eyes caught her by surprise. His fingers moved to her neck, and he pulled her toward him, his mouth hot and hungry on hers.

Quinn knew that every second he wasted increased the already lopsided odds against them. But he allowed himself a deep, lingering kiss. Her hair still smelled faintly of flowers, and her lips were soft. So very soft.

Emotion twisted his gut and fired his blood. He pulled back, his breathing labored. Time had run out.

"We have one thing in our favor. The bastards think we're unarmed." He moved, and suddenly the big black pistol was in his hand. Anne managed to keep from shuddering.

"Are they close enough to shoot?"

"Not yet. I'm going to give them a nice big target. I'm gambling they'll get careless and show themselves." His voice was very quiet, but his tone shivered her skin and brought her gaze homing in on his.

"What kind of target?"

"Me." He took her hand and placed the pistol in her palm. "That's when you empty this sucker at 'em."

Anne looked down at the killing weapon in horror. She had never once fired a gun of any kind. Not even for sport.

"No!" she whispered, her voice catching. "That's suicide. They'll kill you."

"Not if I run fast enough. Aim for the chest. You've got six chances to hit at least one of them. I'm betting you'll get both."

She stared at the gun's trigger. "Don't you have more…more bullets?"

"Yeah, in the saddlebags."

Anne shuddered. Six bullets against two military automatics? There was no way. Quinn would be dead before she managed a single shot. She couldn't let that happen. Not to Quinn.

"We could wait until dark, then sneak away," she said, her words tumbling in her haste to convince him. "It's the dark of the moon now. They won't see us."

She clutched his arm, desperate to keep him safe. He didn't shrug off her touch, but his expression didn't soften, either.

"Anne, these guys know that, too. They won't wait."

As though underscoring his words, the men above let loose with another short volley. Shattered foliage crashed around them, less than a dozen yards above them. Anne held her hands over her ears until the noise stopped.

Next to her, she felt Quinn's body tense. He was ready to make his move. No, she thought. She had to do something. Anything. Oliver women never gave up.

"That's *enough!*" she yelled, her eyes smoldering with anger.

Quinn whipped his gaze toward her, shock mirrored in his dark pupils. "Shut up!" Quinn hissed. "This isn't a game."

Anne ignored him. She was too busy trying to save his life. "*Don't shoot!*" she shouted to the faceless, nameless killers above. "I'm ready to deal."

Silence answered her. Just when she thought she would explode, another Southern voice yelled from above, "Come on up here, sugar, so's we can deal eyeball to eyeball."

"I can't," she shouted back. "I...sprained my ankle. And my friend is unconscious. I think he's dead."

She leaned closer until her mouth was only inches from Quinn's ear. "When they come close, you can shoot them." She shoved the pistol into his hand. "Aim for the chest."

Quinn didn't waste time berating her. Instead, he cocked the pistol and pointed it to the sky.

The silence stretched again, longer this time. Anne could picture the two men straining to see movement below in order to pinpoint her location. And then she heard the furtive sound of large bodies moving through brush.

She bit her lip, praying that she hadn't made a stupid mistake. Finally the rustle of movement stopped, and a voice called, ''We'd be pleased to come on down there to help y'all. Show yourself, sugar, so's we can find you.'' The voice was much closer this time.

Anne's gaze met Quinn's. ''Now what?'' she whispered.

''Tell them you're scared. Tell them you want them to hold their guns over their heads so you'll feel safe.''

''Will they?''

''We'll soon find out.'' He kissed her hard. ''In case I forget to tell you later, I think you're one hell of a woman.''

He maneuvered into a crouch, then signaled to Anne that he was ready. Not a muscle in his big body moved as he waited, his attention focused in the direction of the men's voices. He didn't seem to be breathing. Anne had an impression of great force under rigid control, waiting to be released at precisely the right moment.

''Uh, fellas, how do I know you won't shoot me?'' she called. It wasn't difficult to force the sound of fear into her voice.

''Why, sugar, we was just trying to flush you out, is all.''

The moisture in the ground was seeping through her jeans. Her knees felt clammy. And her hands throbbed where the skin had been ripped away.

Her heart was hammering wildly now, and she couldn't seem to control her breathing. Sweat collected between her shoulder blades, plastering her shirt to her skin.

"Put your guns over your heads so I can see them," she called. "And...and then I'll stand up."

Anne heard the rumble of masculine voices, and then the man called, "Okay, sugar. You got yourself a deal."

Instinctively, she turned to Quinn. He nodded, his eyes cold, his face set.

"As soon as the shooting starts," he whispered, "get down as low as you can. Head that way." He jerked his thumb toward the south. "Town is only three or four miles from here as the crow flies."

Terrified, she stood. Leaves and branches obscured her view, but it didn't take long for her to spot the killers. They were slightly to the right, about seventy feet away, holding their weapons aloft. Was that close enough for Quinn to shoot accurately? she wondered as she pulled the branches aside so that they could see her.

"Here," she called.

The men folded into a crouch, their rifles coming down at the same time. Quinn lunged forward, shoving her behind him as he fired two quick shots. One of the men jerked and fell backward, his rifle silenced.

One down, Quinn thought, running to his left to draw the other man's fire away from Anne. He wasted two shots making sure the man took the bait.

Bullets tore through the flimsy shield of leaves. The man was good, moving as swiftly as Quinn, firing from the hip.

Anne screamed. She called out Quinn's name, tried to get up, but she was trembling so hard she had difficulty coordinating her arms and legs.

Quinn kept running, his heels sinking into the muck. Lead slugs whistled past his head. He headed for a large palm directly ahead, high-powered bullets thudding into the ground behind him.

Ten feet from the tree, he veered, doubling back so quickly the other man was caught off guard. Bullets continued to slam into the ground in front of the tree for a split second, long enough for Quinn to plant his feet and take aim.

His first shot missed. The second one hit the man in the belly just as Quinn felt something slam into his right side. His right leg buckled. At the same time his gun hand went numb.

He sank to the ground. Anne screamed something he didn't understand, and then silence settled. The air smelled of gunpowder and shredded plants.

"Quinn, oh God, Quinn!" Anne cried, running toward the spot where he'd fallen.

He was lying on his back, his eyes open, his big hand still wrapped around the pistol. One knee was bent. The denim covering the thickest part of his right thigh was already saturated with blood. The splotch of red covering his right shoulder was almost as bad.

Anne sank to her knees and began tearing at his shirt. His left hand came up to grip hers. His fingers were hard, but his strength was nearly gone.

"Don't," he ordered, his voice harsh.

"You're hurt," she cried on a sob of fury. "The bastards hurt you."

"Are they...dead?"

Anne cast a swift, shuddering look toward the trampled area where the two men lay twenty feet or so apart. Neither moved. "I think so."

Quinn nodded and closed his eyes for a long instant. Lines of suffering deepened on his face. His skin was slowly draining of color.

"Go," he muttered, his jaw tight. "Hurry. Pilot…will come looking.…"

Fear settled in her stomach like jagged glass. Her face was going numb. "No, I won't leave you."

His eyebrows drew together. Frustration glittered in his eyes. "You can and…you will," he commanded, his voice as cold and empty as a crypt.

"There's something else you should know about Oliver women," she said, her facing growing paler and paler. "We don't take orders worth a damn."

She pulled her hand from his and tugged her shirttail from her jeans. She needed a bandage, pressure, something to stop the bleeding.

Assaulted by pain that threatened the boundaries of his control, Quinn fought to keep the swamping weakness at bay.

"Anne, listen to me." Forcing steel into his voice drained his energy. His breath was coming in shudders now. Pain lanced through his chest like a white-hot blade.

Gritting his teeth, he summoned strength from someplace deep. He forced his mind back, summoning an image of his ex-wife's brittle beauty. He kept Liz's face in his mind, blotting out the sheen of worry in Anne's soft, amber eyes. "Drop the Florence Nightingale act, sweetheart. It's…wasted on me. Just get your cute little fanny down this hill and out of my life, so I can stop pretending to care about you."

"You're hurt…"

"Sweetheart, I've taken worse punishment at the Fourth of July Rodeo and still had enough juice left to screw half the women hanging on me."

The deliberate vulgarity brought a wounded vulnerability to her mouth that seared him worse than the pain of his wounds. But he wouldn't let himself stop. Not while her life was still in desperate jeopardy.

Somehow he managed to block out enough of the agony so that he could sit up. Anne watched him with horror darkening her eyes.

"Quinn, what…?"

He grabbed her by the hair and pulled her toward him. His mouth clamped down on hers, and he savaged her lips until he tasted blood. Hers, his, he wasn't sure.

She whimpered, a wounded, desperate little sound that made him cringe inside.

His right hand didn't want to function. He used his left again, dropping it from a clump of her hair to her breast.

Anne felt his palm grind her nipple without even a hint of his former gentleness. His movements were crude, more like an animal's rutting than lovemaking.

Her mind shouted a denial, but his hand was pulling at her shirt. Buttons tore from their holes. His fingers fumbled with her bra.

Anne struggled, adrenaline giving her enough strength to roll out of his arms.

"Stop it," she whispered, her voice quavering. "You don't mean this. You just…you just want me to leave you. But I won't. I love you."

His mouth twisted. Somehow he found enough strength to run the most important bluff of his life. "Love? C'mon, Anne. You're a big girl. Love is for kids. You and me, we've been around. We're hot for each other, that's all."

Anne stared into his eyes. Sweat beaded his face and tension furrowed his brow, but his eyes were as hard as agate and just as cold. In spite of his wounds, he seemed strong and ready.

"No," she whispered. "I don't believe that's all you felt."

Quinn cupped his groin with his good hand. "C'mon over here, honey," he drawled with a suggestive twist to his hard mouth, "and let me show you what I feel."

Anne felt as though she were drowning. With a muffled cry, she stood up and began to run.

Quinn sat motionless until she was out of sight. Seconds later, the adrenaline that had sustained him began to drain away. He sank back against the ground and closed his eyes, welcoming the sharp, twisting agony taking hold of his body. His one thought before he lost consciousness was of Anne.

Quinn knew he was alive because he hurt. Everything around him was hazy and vague, except the burning agony in his chest. His leg ached like a son of a bitch, too. He seemed to be swaddled in bandages. He couldn't move his right side.

He tried to raise his head to take stock, but the effort was too much. He sank back against the pillow, his head whirling and his stomach lurching. The ceiling was white, and the air smelled of disinfectant. In the distance a muted voice called something over a PA system.

He turned his head slowly to the left. A plastic envelope of some clear liquid was hanging from a shiny metal stand next to his bed, connected to a needle in the back of his hand by clear plastic tubing.

A hospital? he thought. Had something happened?

It took a few moments of fierce concentration before he remembered why he was hurting. He'd been shot.

"Anne." His voice came out as a harsh croak. With his one good hand he struggled to grab the bars keeping him in bed.

"So we're awake," a voice chirped. "About time, I'd say."

The nurse hovering over him was spare and capable-looking, with her salt-and-pepper hair cut in a no-nonsense Dutch bob and kind gray eyes. The hand that counted the pulse in his wrist was warm.

"Did she make it?" he demanded, his voice graveled and weak. His mouth was dry, and his throat hurt, as though someone had jammed something hard down his gullet.

"Easy, Mr. Sinclair. Your pulse is about to set a new world's record. In case you're interested, you've had surgery on your thigh and shoulder," the nurse said with more briskness. "Both will mend, but not unless you relax."

Quinn glowered at her. Even that small movement sent needles of pain through him. "Tell me, damn it," he managed. "Anne. Is she safe?"

"Your friend is fine," the nurse said in a soothing tone. "She was suffering from exhaustion by the time she finally got you down the hill to Madison, but a good night's sleep soon fixed her up."

Quinn closed his eyes and let relief wash over him. Anne was safe. For a beat of time he clung to that thought—until the rest of the nurse's words sank in.

"*She* got me down...the hill?" he asked. "How?"

"On a horse, I understand, slung over the saddle like a sack of oats. How she got you on the horse has to be a story in itself."

The nurse bustled around, checking the various tubes attached to him. Finally satisfied, she poured water into a glass, bent a plastic straw and lifted Quinn's head so that he could take a few sips. The tissues of his mouth were so dry that they seemed to absorb the water before he could swallow.

"Where...?" He started to cough, and pain lanced through his chest.

"In the waiting room. I'll fetch her, shall I?" Without waiting for an answer, the nurse hurried out.

Before Quinn could summon the strength to push himself higher on his pillow, Anne was there, bending over him, her hand clasping his. Her face was pale, her mouth even paler. Her hair was a shiny halo in the light, emphasizing the fragility of her features.

"Hi," she said softly. "We were beginning to think you were going to sleep for a week."

"We?"

Anne sensed the strain in his voice. It was an effort for him to speak. "Ed Franklyn is here, along with an army of guards."

"The Brigade?"

"Ed said to tell you they plugged the leak and not to worry about Meg and the ranch. He has people there, too. Just as you ordered, he said." She tried to force a teasing lilt into her voice, but the past seventy-two hours had stripped her of the last of her resilience.

The desperate search for the horses had taken her nearly a mile up the trail. She had found only one, Sadie. The struggle to get Quinn onto the mare's back had taken all her strength and patience, not to mention Sadie's.

The trip out of the gorge had seemed endless. The

worst, though, had been waiting to find out if he would live or die.

"Damn it, Anne. You could have been killed,'' he managed, trying to touch her face. He discovered that his right arm was immobile, encased in plaster.

"I told you, I'm not much good at taking orders. You'd better remeber that.''

"Oh yeah?''

"Yeah.'' Anne traced the line of his mouth with her fingertip. His normally dark skin was the color of ashes, his jaw covered with stubble. His hair was still matted and tangled.

Quinn was having trouble breathing, but it wasn't pain that was tormenting him. "We need to talk. To…get things straight between us.''

Anne felt a flurry of fear in her stomach. "Not now, Quinn,'' she said quickly. "The nurse said—''

"Now.'' His voice was weak, but it still carried enough force to bring a frown to Anne's face.

His hand gripped hers tighter. "I thought you would be gone by now.''

Anne felt a shiver of hurt move through her. "I couldn't leave until I knew you were out of danger.''

"Am I?''

"Yes.''

She leaned over to kiss him. Her hair fell free of the combs she had used to pull it back, tumbling over his neck. He groaned. Alarmed, she jerked backward.

"Is something wrong?'' she asked.

His scowl deepened. "Hell yes, something's wrong.''

Anne looked around anxiously, her eyes filled with worry. "I'll get the nurse—''

"No nurse. You're my problem.''

"Me?"

Quinn managed a slight nod of his head. "I love you, damn it."

He glowered up at her as though he had just accused her of a heinous crime. Some of the tension pinching inside her eased.

"I know."

"You know?" he muttered, his voice gaining strength. Just being near Anne was the best medicine. "How could you know? I just figured it out myself."

Outwardly Anne beamed, but inside she was shaking. As gently as she could, she sat on his bed and entwined her fingers with his. "While you were unconscious, they wouldn't let me see you. I had to do something or go crazy, so I developed the pictures I took of you."

"Pictures?" he repeated slowly, as though he couldn't quite believe what he'd heard. His lips were dry, and he ran his tongue over them. It didn't help much.

"Yep. My camera was still on Sadie's pommel. Most of my film was in my saddlebags."

"So you...developed them?"

Anne nodded. "They're darn good, of course. But the best ones are of you. The first ones aren't as good, of course, but that was before you fell in love with me."

She felt his fingers tremble, and his eyes grew stormy. "I'm broke, Anne. Everything I have is mortgaged."

"I see." She pursed her lips. "You think I would only want you if you're rich."

He inhaled deeply, then winced at the hot stab of

pain. "No, that's not what I think, damn it. I'm trying to tell you why it would never work between us."

Her eyes were soft and steady on his. He wanted to look away. He couldn't.

"Quinn, stop fighting it. We belong together. I love you. You love me. The camera doesn't lie."

"The hell it doesn't," he muttered, tightening his fingers on her. "It's ridiculous, you and me. I would make your life hell."

Anne lifted her free hand to his face and brushed back the tangled hair. "Probably."

"You're too stubborn for your own good."

"Yes."

"We'll fight."

"Definitely." She let her fingers trail down the hard, stubbled plane of his cheek. "And then we'll make up."

Quinn looked into eyes that were cloudy with desire. Something tore loose inside him, like the knot of a noose.

"I tried to make you leave me."

"I know. I figured that out before I even ran far enough to get out of breath. But I figured you wouldn't fuss as much if you thought I was on my way down the mountain."

His mouth tightened. "I don't fuss," he groused.

"No, you grumble and grouse and order me around like one of your *paniolos*."

She leaned forward and touched her mouth to his. He groaned and his hand came up to trap her. "Damn it, I need you, you crazy woman." The words shuddered from him, bringing a rush of tears to her eyes.

"And I need you."

His mouth found hers. Excitement jolted through her. Soon they were both breathing hard.

Anne felt a tremor take him and pulled back. "You need to rest."

"Later," he muttered. "When are you going back to the mainland?"

Her eyes clouded. "Ed wants to go tonight. He's found me another place until the trial."

"Good idea."

"I want to stay here." Anne tried to nuzzle closer, but he stopped her.

"No. You'll go."

"Quinn—"

He pulled her down for a long satisfying kiss before whispering, "I need time to get used to the idea of getting married again."

Anne's mouth opened, then closed. "I...are you proposing to me?"

Quinn gave a snort. "Son of a gun, I think I am. Must be the pain pills."

Anne let the happiness trapped in her bubble out in laughter. She kissed him this time, then said in a saucy tone, "I accept, on one condition."

"What's that?"

"That I can take as many pictures as I want during my honeymoon."

Quinn groaned and closed his eyes. "I think I'm in big trouble here."

Anne giggled, caressing his face. "You want to have something to show our children, don't you?"

He opened his eyes, his throat clogged with a lump that felt suspiciously like tears. "Children?" he managed.

"Mmm. Maybe not eleven, like old Josiah. But two or three. If you're willing, that is."

For a long moment, Quinn was afraid to speak. A man didn't like to show his vulnerability to the woman he adored. "I'm willing," he said finally.

"There's one more thing you ought to know. Oliver women make terrific mothers."

After that, neither spoke.

Epilogue

Wearily, Quinn climbed the steps of the porch, slapping his hat against his hip to shake off the red dust. It was past twilight, and he was bone-tired from a day in the saddle. Hunger growled in his belly, and his throat was dry.

Another *kona* wind snatched at the palm fronds and bent the slender trunks. At the top of the steps, he paused to take another look at the rolling green pastures. Horses grazed in the paddock beyond newly painted fences. The cattle were settling for the night.

He waited, but the contentment he should be feeling refused to come. For a week now, since the end of Draygon's trial, he'd been restless and on edge.

Now that the Brigade's leader and his cohorts, including the mercenary informer on Franklyn's staff, were safely behind bars, now that the Brigade itself was in disarray and no longer a threat, there was no valid reason for Anne to remain on the mainland.

Still, she hadn't set a date to return to Hawaii.

"Soon," she'd said when he had called. There were so many things to do. Sell her town house, make arrangements for her goods to be shipped, her schedule of obligations to be rearranged.

Automatically, he turned his gaze toward the east. The sky was crowded with dark clouds. What if she didn't come? What if their four months apart had changed her mind? What if she'd decided that a poor rancher and a quiet life in the islands weren't enough for her?

Not that he would put chains on her. He wouldn't. No one had the right to rein in a talent like hers. She would come and go on her trips, and he would be waiting.

If she hadn't decided that the feeling she had for him wasn't really love after all.

Fear knotting his belly, Quinn turned and walked into the old house. It was quiet. Meg and the tourists were down by the pool, winding up another luau. He could hear the ukeleles in the distance.

Shoulders slumped with more than fatigue, he took the stairs one at a time. He was halfway up the first flight when he realized he wasn't alone.

Anne was standing on the landing, in the spot where countless Sinclair wives had waited for their husbands.

"It's about time you got home," she said, the smile he loved trembling faintly. "I was about to saddle Sadie and go out looking for you."

"Were you?" Quinn flung his hat toward the peg by the door. It missed, but he didn't notice. His gaze was fixed on the welcoming glow in her eyes.

"You work too hard," she murmured.

"I'm the boss. It's my job."

"Part of your job, my darling. The other part is loving me."

Anne saw the flash of surprise in his eyes. He hadn't believed in her, she thought. In their love. Perhaps he still didn't. But he would, she thought with a small sweet shiver of anticipation. Oh yes, my darling. It may take me fifty years, but I'll take the pain from your eyes.

Quinn reached the landing and swept her into his arms. She was soft and warm and smelled like the woman he worshipped. His kiss was hungry and yet sweetly tender. Anne pressed closer, enchanted all over again by the feel and taste and scent of him.

Her island cowboy. Her man.

"Welcome home, Ms. Oliver," he said when the kiss ended.

Anne smiled as she caressed his careworn face. "Mrs. Sinclair to you," she murmured. "Or have you forgotten that an Oliver woman always gets what she wants?"

"Thank God," he muttered before lifting her high off the floor into his arms. Anne wondered if old Josiah was watching. She hoped so.